The Midnight Moon

Patricia Warner

Contents

PROLOGUE

The shaman shook his head slowly, his expression grave. The newborn baby was still on the bed, sleeping soundly. "I am sorry, but like the child a few years ago, she cannot stay."

"But--" The distraught mother could barely whimper. The tent was silent, except for the magical broth that churned, used to check the newborn's birth. The broth was swirling in inky darkness, which was a rare, cursed sign. The mother pleaded again, this time in anguish and pain, "Please! Please just let her live!"

The shaman shook his head again.

"Tonight is the twenty-ninth day since her birth, by the thirtieth day she must disappear," The shaman slotted a piece of paper of her name into the newborn's little tunic, "Bring her into the mountains, over the river, anywhere she could be placed at. For the safety of the Village, just bring her away."

The mother grabbed the newborn and rushed out of the tent. Outside, the calmness and silence soothed her, but only momentarily. She had a job to do, not only to send the child away but to make a deal.

In the newborn's tunic, on the piece of paper, a name was scrawled onto it: FERHIA. The mother bounded into the woods, heavy breathing echoing in the stillness of the night.

When the day came, and the mother returned, life carried on but the infant was nowhere to be seen.

***

Along the gushing river and under the silver glare of the faint moonlight, the infant woke, her deep blue eyes staring up at the sky, white and misty. Not far away from her, a pack of wolves stared at the newborn infant, and on top of the Alpha of the Pack, a boy not older than five sat.

His eyes still fixated on her, he whispered something inaudible to the other wolves into its ears, and it nodded, shifting its rather massive head up and down slowly. Padding nimbly to where the awakened newborn was, it grabbed the tunic gently with its teeth and turned back to the pack, leaving the riverbank...

Chapter 1

"K ilfer!" Ferhia yelled to the opposite side of the river, where the scrawny tanned boy some five years her elder was. He turned, and clutched tightly in his hands was a huge bass, large enough to feed two wolves for dinner. Kilfer paddled over to Ferhia, "This catch is enough, little sister. Time to get back."

"I am not little," Ferhia showed a sign of annoyance, but Kilfer simply ignored it with a slight grin on his face.

Above the river, upon the riverbank a wolf stood almost motionlessly, its deep blue eyes fixated on the duo. Finally, it leaped down in a single fluid motion onto the riverbank.

"The Alpha's calling us up, we'd better go," Although Ferhia did not know wolf tongue, she did know that it meant that they should be about ready to leave the river. Kilfer followed, and they climbed out of the water, their tunic wet and heavy, their feet also stained with grime and soil.

Kilfer leaped onto the back of the Alpha and they left, Ferhia trailing behind. Kilfer seemed like a wolf more than a human totally -- with the courage, grace, and strength of the Alpha, as if he was part of the pack -- and she was not.

The forest deepened and the ground steepened as they trailed up the mountain, the Alpha leaping up crevices and ledges while she struggled to keep up, meanwhile trying not to drop the bucket of fish. Sometimes the Alpha would pause and turn back to wait for Ferhia, but most of the time it bounded forward, leaving Ferhia struggling to catch up.

Ferhia's feet hurt as she trudged up the mountain, occasionally twigs and branches underneath her foot would scratch her, and although it happened rarely she would wince each time it scraped her bare soles. Watching Kilfer and the Alpha together in front of her, it made her feel... excluded. Although she tried not to think about it, the Pack and Kilfer always ate together, hunted together and were together, like a family. Yet she was never thought as one family. The wolves hate her presence, and Kilfer would spend more time with the Pack than her.

'The pack has not yet accepted me,' Ferhia thought. She had many dreams, of the pack biting her, flinging her limp body into the river. She knew that it could not possibly happen when Kilfer is still alive, at least, but dreams have meanings.

Ferhia tried to keep these disturbing thoughts to herself and carried on, and finally, after an hour of walking, the forests opened to bare land and the Lair finally came to view. The huge cave was at least thrice the height of even the huge statue of the Wolf God outside the cavern, and as they trod out to the open, above them leading to the cave hundreds of wolves' heads extended out to welcome them, and when they peered out of the ledge beneath them to the horizons miles and miles of land extended out, bathed under the warm glow of the sun.

"Ferhia," Kilfer turned back to her, "Thanks for helping to carry the fish, I will help tomorrow."

"You never do," Ferhia rolled her eyes and dropped the bucket on the stone floor.

"Anyway," Kilfer ignored her, "We need to prepare dinner for the pack, they must be starving."

"And today is your turn to do it," Ferhia mentioned quickly, grinning, "You swore you would prepare dinner yesterday."

"Fine," Kilfer frowned and ruffled the fur of a she-wolf, peering at the direction of the Table, where different coloured berries of different shapes and sizes, and fish were placed on the table, with an entire dead pig dragged back by three canines.

'Great,' Kilfer muttered, 'Now I have work to do.'

Chapter 2

The moonlight shone through the entrance of the cavern, providing them with the only source of light as the pack tore at the raw meat intemperately while Ferhia and Kilfer ate silently.

Her thoughts wandered to elsewhere as she ate the fish. Fifteen days later she would be fourteen, and for that, even Kilfer started shunning away from her, and when she asked why he simply answered, 'Inauspicious year for ya.'

Kilfer strode towards the pack and they turned, welcoming him and leaving Ferhia alone by herself. She seemed together with the pack, but was in fact alone, different from Kilfer and the wolves. She seemed like an oasis in the dry desert, an island in a vast sea, a single star in an empty sky. She was within them, but she was different; at least the Pack treated her as an outsider.

Ferhia glanced at the altar, a small house with a statue of the Wolf God inside it. Three candles flickered in front of the little house, the silhouette of the house flickering in the darkness.

It gave her confidence every time she stared into the yellowish glow.

"Ferhia," Kilfer sat beside her, jolting her out of her thoughts, "Lonely?"

Ferhia did not answer for a while and continued staring at the flames. Kilfer saw where her gaze was locked upon and turned back to her, "Sure you do seem lonely."

"Now you have finally realized," Ferhia finally turned, looking straight at Kilfer's bloodshot eyes.

Kilfer wanted to say something, then he paused realizing that something was not right with Ferhia but finally spoke, choosing his words carefully, "I know that you're angry about me because you feel excluded. I really have no choice, for something would be about to happen--"

Kilfer caught his words suddenly and fell silent, and Ferhia did not speak. It was clear he was keeping something from her. Something that she ought to know, something ominous. The duo sat there for a few awkward moments before Kilfer looked away, sighing, "I cannot say much about this, but I received a vision about you -- and that can't be avoided."

Ferhia sat up straight, looking at Kilfer suspiciously. Not once in her life did Kilfer mention anything about a vision about her, and this time it seemed like an ominous one.

"What'd you mean?"

"I can't tell you much now, but try to stay away for the Pack for now. No matter how hard the truth is, I have to tell you this -- you don't belong here."

Kilfer walks back to the pack, leaving Ferhia stunned. You don't belong here. Kilfer's words stung her hard, deep into her mind and heart. She sat, staring at the candles, but her mind was numb.

Chapter 3

"Look, they are having so much fun," A voice whispered in her head. On the screen, the Alpha cornered Kilfer on a wall. The wolf's eyes were deep red, and Ferhia could see within. The hatred, the bitterness and the wanting for revenge. The canine inched closer, snarling, and leapt forward.

Ferhia did not dare to open her eyes, but there was warm, thick fluid running down her face. She opened her eyes, the Alpha was already on Kilfer. On her face was the blood of her brother. The leader of the pack. Kilfer.

The wolf turned, its blood red eyes staring at her, nailing its eyes right into her soul. She felt small, weak, and could be gnarled to pieces between the wolf's teeth. "Yes, my dear," The voice spoke, this time even more menacing, "Slaughter her."

Then, the last vision she saw was the canine's razor teeth clamping down on her, and the next thing was darkness.

***

Ferhia woke up, her face filled with beads of sweat, her mouth chattering and her heart pounding so hard against her chest. The pack was gone (Ferhia assumed they went to forage for prey in the night), and Kilfer was just awake, cleaning the bust of the Wolf god.

"Kilfer," Ferhia spoke, and he jumped, slightly but enough for Ferhia to notice.

"Uh, yeah?" Kilfer mumbled, turning and standing.

"Where's the pack?" Ferhia averted the conversation, pretending not to see Kilfer's reactions.

"They went to the river, it's their time to catch fish, let's get the berries today," Kilfer shrugged, placing the bust back to its original position in the tiny house, "We'll have breakfast first before we leave."

Ferhia could feel the annoyance in his voice -- he hated getting the berries in the forest for it was filled with danger even when the sun was glaring overhead for it was filled with ferocious animals that killed and ate men calmly, and only with the Alpha they could be guranteed safety. The last time they had met a venomous snake, and it was not a good encounter at all.

They ate in silence, and once or twice a hawk screeched overhead but they did not even mind. When Kilfer raised his head finally, the Pack had just returned. The Alpha nuzzled its snout against Kilfer in affection as Ferhia watched in silence.

"Let's go to get the berries, we don't want to reach the forest later than midday," Kilfer turned to Ferhia. They gathered their tools and left, Kilfer riding the Alpha and as usual, Ferhia trailing behind.

The trees thickened, and darkness set over them; only a ray of light emerged from the tiny holes between the branches. It was silent, and except for the soft padding of the Alpha's foot and the occasional bird tweets and the flutter of wings.

Suddenly, the Alpha paused in front of her, creeping behind the bushes. Ferhia followed, and between a thin crevice, a multicoloured plant with white leaves stuck out of it.

"The... Plant of God," Kilfer marvelled at the beauty of such a rare plant. Every century, only a single plant grew in the most desolate parts of the forest, "How is it even possible to grow here?" Ferhia frowned, "This might be--"

Before Ferhia could finish her sentence, a creature emerged from between the bushes, its horns huge and splattered with red blood.

"Boar plants, as I guessed," Ferhia took a step back. She knew that it was mostly impossible for the Plant of God to grow there, but she knew that the plant would be a boar plant, which the boars would use it to attract its unlucky prey. Kilfer leapt off the wolf's back as it growled, its gaze held on the incoming foe. Both animals glared savagely at each other as the duo stood behind the Alpha.

"R'you je wolf child?" The boar spoke through its thoughts with a heavy accent as it met Kilfer's gaze. He was one of the few who could communicate through animal tongue but was surprised that the boar could speak wolf tongue.

'You speak wolf tongue?" Kilfer raised his eyebrows, but heard the Alpha's voice telepathically, 'Don't listen to him. He is trying to hypnotize you--"

Before the Alpha could finish his sentence the boar charged towards the Alpha, his thick tusks ready to deal a fatal blow to the wolf, but it leapt aside and rammed into the boar from the side. The duo spiralled into the thicket downhill, and Kilfer could feel the pain of both animals as twigs and branches whipped across their bodies.

"Is the Alpha alright?" Ferhia stood at the edge of the thicket, trying to find any sign of movement from below, but the misty air had covered the bottom of the hill.

"He is. I can still feel his presence," Kilfer made a pulling action with his hands and the trees swayed towards him, and soon the Alpha was brought back up.

"Impressive, young Kilfer. But we should beware of those boars," The Alpha padded towards them. Kilfer smiled and nodded with a sense of appreciation. Even Ferhia was surprised that Kilfer could control plants, something more powerful than simply wind.

As they tread downhill, plucking mangoes and pears and bunches of other fruit the scenery below could be seen, the rivers flowing smoothly, cascading down a huge waterfall to a huge lake, and beyond that was acres of sparse land and little towns and villages were scattered forth. Ferhia averted her gaze to her brother, who clung to a tree, tugging at a fruit and it came off from its branches. Kilfer never let her venture anywhere further than the waterfall.

"Ferhia, catch this!" Ferhia turned and from high up Kilfer flung a mango at her. She lept up and caught it mid-air, and placed it into the basket.

"Great," Kilfer clambered down from the tree swiftly, and hauled the basket up, "It's a good amount of fruit, time to leave for home." They left, but as they walked up the mud caked lane Ferhia knew one day, that one day she would do her own exploration by leaving the mountains to faraway lands.

Chapter 4

A lone figure stood before the altar of the Wolf God, a silhouette cast upon the small house as the silvery glow of the moonlight lit up the cavern. He glanced backward furtively and saw his sister and the Pack were still asleep.

He started to chant, feeling his deep connection to nature and the Wolf God start to form. A cold gust blew from his back that made him shiver, and in front of him the warm glow of the flames from the candle warmed him up.

Kilfer paused abruptly in his chants, and flames and wind stopped, the candles stamped out by something he could simply feel, but not see.

A vision, Kilfer felt his mind getting dizzy, and the surroundings morphed around him, getting dimmer and dimmer until it changed entirely.

***

Kilfer was alone, frozen in a sea of glass, the isolation hurting him so much his mind throbbed and he shut his eyes tight. He could not move, not even expel the slightest whisper from his mouth. Then he felt a movement, a slight tremor in the glass that he opened his eyes slowly.

Outside the glass that he was confined within, a girl walked towards him and swiped her palms on the glass, and the glass turned clear. Ferhia. It was Ferhia, but her eyes were closed, motionless, like an empty case, but inside was nothingness. Then, a drop of blood surfaced up from her forehead, hovering in front of him.

Then, the surroundings changed around him. He was moving so quickly through a myriad of colors, his entire body felt weightless until he was flung back into reality...

Kilfer hit the ground hard, his body reeling from the impact. He was back again, and the silence of the night soothed him, but his heart was still palpitating from the vision. Kilfer turned towards Ferhia where she was sleeping, and the pack showed no sign of movement. Sighing deeply, he turned back to the altar and continued his chants...

***

Ferhia woke. Staring up through the hole at the top of the cavern into the pitch darkness of the night sky, the calmness of the unknown embraced her. What was beyond this land? Even higher than she could jump, higher than this mountain, even higher than the clouds that block what lay beyond the sky -- so high that she could see it but yet could not grope it. The little sparkles of light glowing vibrantly in the night sky, reminding her of the days of her own before she turned eleven when she lay on the ground every evening with Kilfer. She remembered the night she turned eleven, she heard a shout outside the Lair, but she was too afraid to check what happened, but she simply knew that something happened, something that she did not know, and she supposed she did not want to know.

She turned around, and could not find where Kilfer was. A shadowy movement drifted past her eyes, and she whipped around to the huge carved statue of the wolf god, and on its right paw on the altar, a figure knelt, chanting phrases in Wolf tongue. He was like a silhouette shrouded in the darkness, his eyes closed and he was shuddering, his face contorted in grief and agony and his fists held tight.

The candle was lit, stumped, then lit multiple times again by an unknown force. "No, no, no..." Kilfer managed a deep strangle before an unseen force pushed him off from the ground onto the stone floor. He stood, shaking, then Ferhia shut her eyes tight and pretended to sleep while Kilfer turned to look at her. But when Kilfer turned back to the chants, unnoticed to him a pair of brown human eyes was staring at him...

Chapter 5

"Ferhia," Kilfer's voice rang in her head.

Ferhia woke up and saw Kilfer standing above her, peering down. Behind him, the sky was still a shade of dark purple, it was not yet dawn.

"I want to show you something," Kilfer whispered, "Follow me."

Kilfer darted swiftly past the pack who was asleep, but as Ferhia walked past them she was careful not to get too close, for her presence always made them wary, and now they would growl at her as if she was some sort of evil omen.

They walked, their bare feet taking slow and silent steps across the stone floor. Finally, Kilfer stopped behind the statue of the wolf god, the towering figure in the middle of the Lair. Behind it was smooth, gray stone with ancient runes that were carved by the human leaders of the Pack long ago.

"I am going to show you something, that I believe the time is ripe to show it to you now," Kilfer brushed his hands over the cold stone lightly, and paused his hands over a small circular carving on the wall, that, Ferhia supposed, was a rune in the shape of a square with intricate carvings. Then he pressed the rune, and the entire wall of writing was broken into two parts, slowly opening.

"What is this? I've never seen it before," Ferhia gazed into the darkness of the secret passage in awe, but Kilfer placed a finger on his lips.

"We don't want the Alpha to catch wind that I showed you this. They do not like you, I am sure you know about this that they are shunning away from you. But we have more important matters to talk about, about your appearance and the fate of the pack," Kilfer directed her to the stairs that led down to the darkness, "If it pleases you to come with me, sister."

They descended into the darkness, the staircase seemed endless as they trod down, far away continuous drip-drops of water echoed off the walls. When Kilfer paused they had reached a passageway, where the stairs finally ended.

Weird runes, weirder than the writing of the wolf tongue was scrawled on both walls, differing in sizes and shapes.

"This is the writing of the first human leader of the Pack, about a millennium ago," Kilfer turned to Ferhia, grinning, "These were the prophecies of the first human leader of the Pack, Mizervon the Ancient. Not only did he have memories, but prophecies was what he wrote, inscribed in the old wolf tongue, including the famine a century and a half ago. The wolves told me Mizervon died at an age of eighty-three, but when he did no one knew, and he might not have died..."

Seeing Ferhia staring intently at Kilfer, wanting him to continue, he changed the topic, "Now, Ferhia, there is a prophecy told by him. And it would be happening on you -- and it matters to the survival of the pack."

Locking his gaze on a section of the runes he translated aloud:

A millennium later all shall cease to breathe A millennium later the fall shall dawn A millennium later the wrath of a caged demon shall send the world to raze Fear him you shall

All for the survival of a child All for the sacrifice But the price shall be great.

When he finished speaking, the only thing they heard was the continuous dripping of water and the echoes of the last line of the prophecy.

"The price shall be great... price shall be great...be great...g reat...a..."

The last echoes faded into the darkness, and Ferhia found out that she had been staring at Kilfer all the while. Slowly, she piped up, "What does it mean?"

"Who knows?" Kilfer shrugged, "These prophecies are confusing, who knows what it might really mean? But I do know that it is a prophecy about you."

Kilfer fell silent and seemed to be hiding something from her. "So...how did you know?"

But Kilfer did not reply, and stared at the runes, unwilling to look her in the eye. Ferhia waited for awhile, then stood and clambered swiftly up the carved uneven steps, leaving Kilfer alone in the dark...

Chapter 6

"Ferhia," Something cold touched her lightly.

"Stop it Kilfer, I want to sleep," She mumbled and turned away.

"Ferhia," The voice hissed again, this time harsher and the touch on her bare skin sent ripples of pain through her, jolting her and she woke, coming face to face with... nothing. She could feel its presence, but it was far away yet its voice seemed right in front of her face. From the ground, a small gust of wind threw the leaves into a dance, while from the entrance to the Lair dark mists surged in.

Her eyes met Kilfer's, who was also staring at the dark mists, aghast. Whatever it was, Ferhia knew, it was not a good thing.

The wolves were raised from their slumber, but their eyes were closed and legs drooping as they were hauled by a force unseen to the eye several feet into the air. From their white fur, the stain of dark red blood emerged, drenching their lifeless bodies.

"What have you done?" Kilfer screamed at the dark mist as the lifeless canines flopped to the ground. Yet Ferhia was in a daze. Everything happened in a few moments' time, she did not know why it happened at all.

"Meet me at the Swamps and I shall revive the Pack. If not, their bloodline ends this day!" A voice boomed from above as the mist turned to nothingness. Then what followed was an annoying silence as they stood there for a long time.

Silently, Kilfer dragged his feet towards the Alpha, limp and lifeless. She could feel Kilfer's vengeance, and his contorted emotions blew a cold, strong gust of wind from outside the cave. His fists were shaking, but just then did Ferhia realize that Kilfer's vengeance... was directed at her.

Kilfer knelt before the canine in its warm blood as Ferhia tottered towards him blindly.

"Don't come near me," She heard Kilfer say in her mind, but she continued taking slow steps towards him.

"I said stop," She could feel Kilfer's annoyance, but something drew her closer.

"I said stop!" Kilfer yelled suddenly with a tone of finality, nailing Ferhia to the ground with a strong, sudden gust, leaving her dazed

"What did I do?" Ferhia frowned, suddenly realizing how dry her mouth was.

"It was a mistake to bring you here. You are a cursed child, damned for eternity!" Kilfer stood over her in contorted rage,

"I hoped, for all the years you came to the pack. I hoped you were not the person in the prophecy! But it turns out I was wrong."

Then the wind subsided, and a cold draught washed over her as she continued looking at Ferhia. There were too many emotions in Ferhia, Kilfer, and both of them intertwined. Then, Kilfer finally spoke, this time softly with a tinge of regret as he lay his back on the statue of the Wolf God, "It's alright. The prophecy is the prophecy, it is already over. What we can do now... is to revive the pack, and to go to the swamps."

Everyone within a hundred miles from here knew that the Swamp was a place that all the living would avoid, but the more they avoided it, the more powerful the dark forces within the Swamp swelled, only restrained by the curtain that held them back.

Ferhia raised her gaze to the west, which was the directions to the Swamps. However, besides the plains and forests and small villages that filled the land beneath them, beyond that was simply white mists blanketing what lay ahead.

Then, she caught sight on a tiny reddish spark glowing beneath the mountain. It was unclear, but in the darkness of the night, it seemed like a flicker of life -- except that Ferhia noticed that it meant... death. "Kilfer!" She turned back and cried, before scampering to the ledge. A huge village was ablaze with the flames flickering in the darkness, a reddish madness seemingly seeping the lifeforce of all that was in the village.

"Your curse," Kilfer did not even wince, staring calmly at the buildings, some partially standing but other smaller ones burnt completely to the ground, "I had visions from the Wolf God before. All that you loved, all you once adored so deeply and dearly, and even all that you knew -- will be gone, just because of the curse. And it should include me, but I do not know why I survived."

Kilfer and Ferhia sat in silence as they watched the blazing flames. Both of them knew -- but did not say -- that in the midst of the destruction in the village there might be the burning corpse of her parents, but it was too late.

Maybe, Ferhia thought, she might not be able to meet her parents again after all.

Chapter 7

"So, are you really planning to leave for the Swamps? It is dangerous, it might be a trap," Ferhia scowled at Kilfer's decision.   "What... singing, dancing... what is that even?" Ferhia's frown deepened even further, and Kilfer shrugged, "Never mind that, you'll see for yourself later."

"That's the only way," Kilfer strode ahead of her as they passed by thickets and trees. A distance away, the gushing of fast-moving waters of the river echoed like a soothing lullaby in Ferhia's consciences as they continued downstream. "Just follow the river," Ferhia remembered Kilfer say. It led from the Lair, and leading so far downstream it now seemed endless, even though she walked down the same pathways every day.

Finally, after both her feet felt like lead and the weight of their supplies heavy on her shoulders they paused. The sounds of the water had subsided, and they had come to a cliff, so steep only the birds and bees could build their homes on them. Ferhia had never imagined she would feast her eyes on such a majestic beauty, of the light green pastures rolling on the fields, men, women, and children were wandering amongst them, villages and towns with towering towers and huge structures rising high above the ground, that Kilfer had called buildings. Near to them, the river flowed down the cliff, and beneath them it landed onto the lake, the waters silent and clean.

Meanwhile, Kilfer's eyes were focused on the distance, his face solemn and calm. "Ferhia, we have to leave now," Kilfer turned towards her, then rested his gaze upon the fast-flowing rivers.

"But...how? I mean, it's the cliff from here," Ferhia took a quick glance at the cliff, "We can't just climb down."

"No we're not, Ferhia," Kilfer walked past her to the river-banks, and placed his fingers into the water, letting it rush between them, "Look."

Ferhia stared into the water, and moments later a wave of water rose out of the fast-moving river, circling him, raising him into the air. "Come; Ferhia, let's ride the waves!" Kilfer yelled above the noise of the waves and extended his hand out. Ferhia grabbed his hand tightly and hauled her up onto the gathering wave he had created from the force of nature.

The water felt cold as they descended down the waterfall, Ferhia crouched behind Kilfer above the water he had created, and for a moment she felt so light and the wind kissed her cheeks so gently -- until she landed into the lake below. It hit her and Kilfer hard, her eyes stung so much she had to keep them closed and even in that state she had to prevent herself from drowning until a pair of hands hauled her into the air and onto solid ground.

"K...Kilfer, what happened?" Ferhia sat, shivering on the ground and dabbing her eyes. Even though she had herself submerged in the water, that was the first time she had felt the cold dragging her down.

"That was a tiny error, mistakes do happen," Ferhia could see that Kilfer tried not to meet her gaze and was suppressing his laughter, and it was then did Ferhia realize how unkempt she appeared. Ferhia gave him a murderous stare and Kilfer stopped laughing. "Fine, ill stop," Kilfer raised a hand and warm gust of wind was carried towards them, and finally Ferhia stopped shaking.

When they reached the village nothing was left but smoke and the ruins of buildings. The walls were covered with leaves, and there was no sign of life there, it seemed like a living hell.

Ferhia walked with caution, and with every step she took the leaves cracked beneath their feet, burnt white bones were strewn all over.

"So, how do you know that it is my birth village?" Ferhia whispered to Kilfer as the avoided stepping onto the bones.

"I can feel it, you are so connected to this place, even though you have lived in the Lair for almost your entire life you still are inseparable from your birthplace," Kilfer said, then frowned, "Don't you feel it too?"

Ferhia nodded, but in fact, she felt nothing at all.

***

It was already nearing dusk, the duo had not found anything related to the death of the Pack, or who was her parents. One thing was clear: The village's fire and the death of the Pack was a single curse, and to find out who did it they had to venture into the Swamps. Yet it was already too dark for them to continue.

"Come, Kilfer that village is the closest place for us to go," Ferhia jabbed at the dim lights ahead, treading through the thick weeds, "Let's see if they allow us to stay there for a night."

As soon as Kilfer and Ferhia found their way out of the weeds they heard an old man call out, "Hey, who are you?"

Ferhia turned, and that was the first human besides Kilfer that she ever saw in her entire life. He was not very tall, barely the height of Kilfer and his hair was the color of salt. The tunic he wore was very odd-looking and bore totally no resemblance to what Kilfer wore, and with his outlandish accent, he seemed totally alien to Ferhia.

Yet, Kilfer never seemed to bother about his appearance and conversed with him in the same accent that Ferhia could barely understand. Finally after quite a long conversation that Ferhia could simply understand a few words, the old man nodded and entered the village gates. Kilfer beckoned towards her and they entered the village.

That was the first time Ferhia saw so many people, men, women, children all streaming across the huge, wide streets, buildings of all shapes and sizes piled high up like magic. But when they entered all of the people stopped what they were doing and stared at them for a moment, then continued what they were doing, with some turning to glance at them.

"They're just not accustomed to strangers, Ferhia," Kilfer whispered into her ears as they followed the old man down the bustling lane, "It's alright, you will see that they are quite welcoming later, don't be afraid."

Ferhia could only manage a tiny nod, but said nothing as they walked on, partially aware that they were heading on to a huge building, on the walls outside were pieces of glass attached to the walls fitting perfectly, some wide opened and some tightly shut.

As they entered the building a whiff of cold air stung all over her, but this was not the cold wind she had experienced that made her huddle up every night, but a gentle touch of a cool wind that revitalized her, and she had never felt that kind of feeling in her entire life.

The entire building was filled with the cool wind, and Ferhia was still staring intently around the granite walls and pillars when the old man halted in front if them. "Here comes a visitor," Ferhia heard the old man say, and turned. He was speaking to a young man barely twenty as Ferhia judged, and after a moment the old man turned towards them, "Young travelers, you must be tired. We don't have many travelers who usually pop up at our gates, so we have the best rooms for you to rest. Come, follow Sir Baurette, he will lead you to your rooms."

***

The stairs extended so high up, and with every step, the stairs extended up she could find no blunt edges or uneven surfaces on the stairs and walls. Finally, they reached a door, and it swung in, revealing a room within.

"Here's your rooms, if you have anything to request, just find me just the floor below," The man who was called Sir Baurette showed them their rooms, and left.

Then, Ferhia realized that she was at a loss for words. Everything seemed so unique, almost magical, how in her wildest dreams could there be walls carved out perfectly, and how was there cold air within the buildings? Even the buildings' structures and water flowing out from a hole in the wall seemed so magnificent to her in the first place.

Ferhia was just wanting to turn to ask Kilfer what this is all about, but Kilfer seemed so calm when he spoke, as if he knew about everything here, "I know you have doubts on almost everything here, I came to such a place before for a month when I was nine, you were barely four then. You see, many of these are the creations of humankind, our kind, those that are created by thousands -- even millions of minds over the millennium and beyond."

Kilfer paused, but Ferhia did not speak, so he had to continue, "We would only live here for a night, so try to get comfy, I'm sure you would. Oh, and I am informed just now that they would be having a village celebration later at night, looks like we're lucky."

"What... celebration?" Ferhia frowned at the pronunciation of the word.

"It just a sort of... huge feasts, singing, dancing, and having a great whale of a time there," Kilfer struggled to explain.

Chapter 8

Ferhia had never seen such a dinner before, it was a huge feast, hundreds of tables lined up beside one another, meat and berries of all kinds and those that she had not seen before placed on fine porcelain plates, and glasses of liquid Ferhia did not know what it was. Hundreds of candles lit up the streets and everyone was 'dancing', as Kilfer described while Ferhia jostled uneasily through the crowd, Kilfer following close behind.

"Ferhia," Kilfer grabbed a bunch of grapes from a plate and continued following Ferhia, "Do you like it?"

Ferhia paused, and turned, not knowing what to say. "Un-accustomed, maybe," Ferhia finally groped for a word to say, "But Kilfer, remember that we really have to leave tomorrow by sunrise, it's better to rest early." She turned back to the inn which they would rest for the night, then back to Kilfer.

"Nah its fine," Kilfer popped another grape into his mouth, "Just tonight, a night of pleasure shall suffice."

They continued strolling (maybe jostling through the crowd, which Ferhia did) through the lanes aimlessly, Ferhia's mind deep in thought about her parents. She caused their deaths, and when wanting so dearly to meet them all her life -- the chance was gone.

But here, in this village, she felt that she was back again, back to her own kind, like a wolf pup that finally returned to its own pack. The sense of belonging -- although quite uncomfortable -- seemed greater than anything else. For the first time, she paused and looked around, surveying every human, every building, every glass attached to the wall (Kilfer told her it was called a window), every laughter and every plate of food. For the first time, a smile crept up unknowingly her cheek as she felt the satisfaction rush over her.

"Feelin' better?" Kilfer spoke behind her. Ferhia turned and realized her smile was evident on her face and kept it away immediately from him.

"Don't need to hide that," Kilfer's grin spread wider, "It's natural. I haven't been back with my own kind for so long."

"Hey, two young travelers!" A strangled voice emanated from the corner of a building. They halted their conversation and turned, and there the same old man that had directed them to the inn stood with a young girl barely her age, "Happy here so far?"

"Of course!" Kilfer answered haughtily, "The food is great, eh, Ferhia?" Ferhia did not answer but continued staring at her feet.

"So here is my granddaughter, Alksept," The old man had to clear the tension, "She'll just keep you company for tonight, aye."Alksept stepped forward, yet said nothing.

"Sure thing, more company would be better, I guess," Kilfer grinned, but Ferhia saw in Alksept's eyes something was amiss. As soon as the old man left Alksept gazed up at the duo and spoke a single sentence, "Follow me."

***

"Why are you leading us back to the inn?" Ferhia asked Alksept as they turned back to the street that the inn was. The celebration was still ongoing, people of all ages eating and drinking, some drunk and one half-awake and slumped on a table.

Alksept did not reply but hastened her footsteps even more. Ferhia turned to glance at Kilfer, who simply shrugged and they followed her into the building.

As soon as she shut the door behind them, the noise outside on the streets was muffled, and Alksept turned to them, "Where are you leaving to? Answer me honestly."

None of them spoke, until Kilfer piped up, "The city Eltbough to the North, why do you ask?" Ferhia thought that Kilfer made it up, but Alksept's tone softened, "I thought you were leaving to the marshes, for if you were travelling north, besides Eltbough the Swamps would be your destination. So where d' the two of you come from?"

"Oh," Kilfer raised his eyebrows, "It's really far away from here, the city with glass walls of Erbaulgh we come from." Ferhia glanced at him, but he made no sign to wink at her. How good he is at lying, Ferhia thought, why did I not notice how good he is at lying earlier?"

"Wow," Alksept marvelled, and Ferhia thought that place Kilfer mentioned must be marvellous, "That's such a great place! I wanted to leave for that place too, but grandpa said I am too small to leave for such a distant destination."

"No worries, I'm sure you will get there soon enough. Time flies and soon, who knows, you could leave for Erbaulgh!" Kilfer grinned, turning towards Ferhia for a moment, but she did not realise.

"By the way, what are your names?" Alksept asked, and Kilfer replied, "Kilfer is my name, and Ferhia is her name. By the way, why does this place feel so uncomfortable?" Kilfer glanced up at the opened windows. The air was stale but true enough there seemed to be a sensation quite uncomfortable, like a layer of dust covered over them, it was then that Ferhia realized.

"Yeah," Alksept sighed and slumped onto a couch, "It all happened yesterday, for our proximity to the Swamps, we are all prone to the changes in the dark magic there. And yesterday it all changed. It seemed that they are getting restless, some ancient powers awakening. I don't want to know, but something is happening in there..."

Ferhia turned to Kilfer, and she realized that he was also looking at him, but none said a word.

***

As soon as they returned to their room and Alksept left, Kilfer said, "Your curse, Ferhia. It is happening now. The Swamps is pulling you towards them."

"But... it was not... I did not want..." Ferhia was at a loss for words.

"I understand. But things could not be changed, it's within you the moment you came to this world. It's alright, I don't blame you," Kilfer tried to comfort her, but the wound of words had already been inflicted upon Ferhia. Her eyes were red, and tears were welling up in her eyes. Kilfer decided not to say anything for some time, instead gazing up at the plain white ceiling in silence.

"We will leave at dawn," Kilfer muttered to himself a little too loudly, "The Swamps will be our destination."

Chapter 9

No one spoke a single word as the duo wandered through the forests, the leaves crackling beneath their feet and the heat and silence so annoying. They had left the village at dawn, and after a few hours stopping at rivers and lakes for water and berries, they had been continuously walking.

From afar forest nymphs, the 'Guardians' of the jungle as they knew it leaped around within the thick trees, but Ferhia paid them no attention, and whenever a breeze swayed a few leaves would be blown to the ground, but other than that complete silence took over. Both were on the same paths, but within their minds, they were thinking two different things.

Who are my parents? Ferhia thought. Maybe, one of the burnt bones she stepped upon during their short walk at her birth village was her parents, she did not know.

The pack is dead, Kilfer thought. Ferhia's curse had killed them-- he paused. He knew he must not let thoughts of that pass his mind even the slightest bit, for his connection to nature around him was close, and thinking these negative thoughts would only make Ferhia feel uneasy. It was the darkness at the swamps. Yes, it was, it was neither of their faults. He turned around, Ferhia was still in deep thought herself, totally oblivious to Kilfer's gaze.

Both were engrossed in their thoughts until they felt that the air was colder and misty did they pause to see where they were. The original cobblestone path had disappeared, and the green trees had turned to leafless bones, seemingly a ghastly apparition of a forest. If there was perchance a bird tweet, they would have heard it -- but there was none.

"Where are we?" Ferhia whispered, sensing the change in the atmosphere.

"I don't know, and I don't want to know," Came the short reply, and they took slow steps, and when they peered forward except for the mist and the shrouded view of the trees there was nothing else that she could see, until they made up the shape of a dark cave ahead, barely visible.

"What..." Ferhia whispered to herself, straining her neck to try to see further, but Kilfer padded forward, and Ferhia had no choice but to follow. Finally, they were in front of the cave, the opening was not very huge, the ceiling slightly taller then them and any of them could easily slip through it.

None of them spoke, for they knew well anything could happen anytime but they were no other paths for them, so they had to enter it. The cave widened as they went deeper. Besides their breathing and footsteps, there was no sound at all. The walls gradually shone slightly, Ferhia noticed, and small cracks in the stone shone light from within it, red light on one and blue light on another.

Then, the cave split into two sides, and they paused. Both sides led to a separate tunnel, and both did not seem pleasing to them.

"I think we should go back," Ferhia tapped on Kilfer's shoulder, but Kilfer shook his head, and continued to stare into the darkness where faint glows of blue and red lights spread out from the wall.

"No, I know this place," Kilfer spoke, his voice echoing around the tunnel, "I met it in a vision, I know it. The cave of dreams, it is called as I remember. It gives answers only once to a few once, leave it and you shall not get the answers, possibly your entire lifetime. I have a question I seek, and I am sure you do too, although I do not know what is it, I can feel it, sister. Let us part ways for now, meet me outside this cave when you are done, and this place is sacred, do not think about the Swamps or any damned place after we go past this place."

"But--" Ferhia frowned and wanted to protest, but was stopped by Kilfer.

"It is safe, trust me. The visions would never lie -- they never do."

Watching Kilfer leave, his silhouette getting fainter and fainter as he walked on, Ferhia felt a sense of loneliness. She was all alone now, looking into the other tunnel, the darkness seemed so glaring. But she had to, for the question she might not get the answer her entire life. Taking a deep breath, she hurried into the tunnel.

The entire cavern was filled with mirrors, spreading her reflection all around in a never-ending pattern. Her head hurt for all the mirrors that surrounded her, and she shut her eyes tight, focusing on herself. All the reflections seemed to have a life of their own, trying to tug her lifeforce away from her original body, and she was concentrating to keep her soul within herself.

"Tell me what you seek," A voice, light, and crystal clear echoed in her ears.

"My parents. Who are they?" Ferhia whispered to the voice, and the mirrors changed around her. On the mirror, two shadows appeared, and she took a few slow, deliberate steps forward.

Then, the two shadows fell into a heap of bones before she could reach them, and behind a cloaked figure stood, a knife in his hand. Ferhia could not feel her hands when she pounded on the mirror, but the assailant in the mirror revealed the face beneath the cloak -- and her face was beneath it.

"Your parents," The voice echoed in the hall, "They signed a bond with the darkest of spirits within the Swamps. It saved you from death -- but it came at a price: and it is their death. You killed them. You killed the pack. You are the murderer." The voice silenced itself, and the mirrors returned to their original positions. After that, Ferhia placed her hands lightly on the smooth mirror and knelt down, placing her face on the mirror. The hall remained silent, but at the place on the mirror her face rested on, it was slippery with her tears...

***

Kilfer was afraid.

Even though he had consoled Ferhia that nothing bad would happen, he was still worried as he slid further into the tunnel. Anyway, his visions were not always so straightforward -- he was sure that no physical harm can be inflicted, but about psychological harm, Kilfer did not know.

Then, he paused. What lay in front of him was swirling, boiling lava and the heat was totally unbearable for him. On the other side of the huge cave of lava the Alpha stood on the ledge.

"Tell me what you seek," The Alpha spoke in wolf tongue, but he supposed it might be a way the cave chose to speak to him.

"Who killed the pack?" Kilfer spoke, his voice echoing across the hall. Then, a shadow of a figure materialized from the walls, an axe gripped tightly in its hand, and it plunged the blade deep into the Alpha's throat. There was no noise as the wolf fell, and it faded into the darkness.

The shadow strode nearer, and then Kilfer could finally see the countenance of the shadowy figure.

It was Ferhia.

Chapter 10

No one spoke as Ferhia and Kilfer trod out of the cave, both eyes were red (they knew each other had been in tears but none cared to ask the other about what happened) and both were still trying their best to hold their tears.

Once they emerged, the forest reappeared and it was already day, and it was then that they realised how long they were in there. But something felt different, that there was not the slightest sound of the birds and wind, and the fresh air was getting stale with every single step they took.

Ferhia did notice that Kilfer was suspiciously eyeing her, but paid no heed to him. Instead, she continued on as if nothing had happened.

Meanwhile on the other side of the forest something stirred, a breeze swirling up clumps of dust and leaves, then came a crack beneath the ground, a sound emnated from within:

Come, beloved one. Come, to the deal That your parents paid. A sacrifice A worthless one For til' the end of time To me you shall be. Your curse troth to me To me you shall be. For eternity Thou shalt not be free!

Meanwhile, the duo shuddered lightly -- but it was not because of the cold.

***

Finally, the forest cleared, the damp warm air finally gone, and they breathed in a whiff of the fresh air. They paused, and surveyed the atmosphere. It was just one of the days, Kilfer thought, where they simply sniffed the air to know the direction that they were heading to. Yet now, they were stuck on a cliff, and far away mists and clouds blocked their vision, and the cliff extended so far below, green plains and hills sprawling out for miles and miles far below them.

Far into the mist, hovering in the air was a huge forest, like a clump of ground lifted high above the ground like a massive fist.

"We... climb down?" Ferhia asked, glancing down at the land beneath.

"I don't think we can," Kilfer spoke, glancing down at the steep cliff face. Ferhia could feel that Kilfer was avoiding her gaze, but tried her best not to show that she noticed. "How about this," Kilfer raised an eyebrow, glancing towards the huge clump of earth that was hovering midair, "I do not know why that piece of land is hovering up, but its fine, I guess. Let me try to control it."

Kilfer shut his eyes tight, and used a force of nature he had but Ferhia could not see, trying to tug the massive piece of land towards them. Ferhia was doubtful he could do so, but did not say anything. The huge clump of soil still sat like a huge boulder within the mists, and Ferhia did not know how it came to be so high up the plains beneath.

Her attention was drawn back to Kilfer, who was struggling. Beads of perspiration rolled down from his forehead to the neck, and his veins were starting to pop out of his hands.

Then from the corner of the eye the huge clump of earth move through the misty air towards them, it seemed like there was a mysterious force pushing it towards them, and soon it paused just at the edge of the cliff. Kilfer staggered back, panting and exhausted while Ferhia finally saw how huge thisclump of earth was.

In fact, it was not simply a clump of earth, but an entire hovering forest, and trees and shrubs were draped over the gray rock and brown soil. Ferhia stepped up carefully, aware of how even the huge piece of land trembled under her mere weight, and Kilfer followed suit.

With a pushing motion, Kilfer controlled the rock, this time seemingly effortlessly, and they glided through the air. As Kilfer wrestled the imaginary controls of the rock, Ferhia started exploring the land, but simply besides the lush greenery and the feverish cold, there was nothing that she could see.

Turning back, she saw Kilfer controlling the entire land as if it were a toy. Ferhia had never knew that Kilfer's magic could be so powerful; she had seen him deliver gusts of wind and resurrect a dying tree, but controlling things in such a huge scale was totally breathtaking.

Finally, a huge looming cliff extended out like the front hull of a ship out of the mists, and Kilfer pushed his hands hard onto the ground and it stopped. They climbed out to a ledge, extending deep enough into the cliff face that even five men could stand on it. Not too distant from where they landed, a waterfall glided from the top of the mountain, descending far beneath the mists until Ferhia could not see where it landed, and when they glanced forward, behind the waterfall there was a grotto, a gaping hole twice the height of Kilfer.

"Come," Kilfer said, not even turning his head to glance at Ferhia, but she knew he was too lethargic to carry on with the journey, but something from the corner of Kilfer's eyes told her that it might just not be because of his tiredness that he is avoiding her gaze, "Let's stay here for the night, I need rest."

In the grotto they found some water, a flat slab of stone perfect for a resting spot, and that was it. At night, the sounds of the rushing water woke them with the cold, and when they nearly fell asleep it woke them again until they decided not to sleep.

Ferhia knelt slowly and carefully on the edge of the ledge and saw the water cascade from the top like a line of water, but trapping her, cutting her off from the wind outside like a veil. Then, a bout of water ejected from the waterfall onto Kilfer's hands, and before that she did not realise he was beside her.

"Hi," Ferhia spoke softly, barely audible to have been covered by the roaring of water.

Kilfer gave no response, twirling the water above his hands in boredom.

Ferhia turned back to face the waterfall, and let the roaring of the water cleanse her thoughts, and shut her eyes to listen to every rhythmic clap of the waterfall, drowning her ears within the sounds. After a long time she opened her eyes, and Kilfer was gone. The voices of water had cleansed her senses, and she decided to enter the cave once again. The night was still reigning above the land, and when she stepped in it was pitch black, so dark she could not even see herself, but at the corner lying down Kilfer was muttering prayers, but Ferhia could clearly hear what it was. The prayer, only spoken by mortal beings when they were dying. The verse of the souls.

Ferhia knew, Kilfer had something he hid from Ferhia -- once again.

Chapter 11

Day came, and Kilfer trod out of the cave out to the ledge behind the waterfall, Ferhia trailed quickly behind. The clouds still obscured their view beyond the waterfall, but neither of them paid any attention to the view, for after a sleepless night both were too drowsy to utter a word, let alone start a conversation with each other, but simply trudged along the ledge until they reached a gap along the rock that allowed them to climb up.

"Wait... climb?" Ferhia frowned as Kilfer placed a hand on a jagged edge on the rock.

"Yeah," Kilfer scaled the jagged surface of the cliff face and hauled himself higher and higher, and to Ferhia it seemed effortless.

"We'll ride the wind from here," Kilfer reached the top, which was barely a couple feet up. Ferhia reached the top, scraping her knees halfway but it simply hurt with a dull throb.

Kilfer raised himself up to the sky and raised her up. For a moment, Ferhia felt so light -- almost weightless -- as both of them flew up to meet the wind.

To the south, the sky was still dim with the first rays of sunlight cascading down on the forests and plains and mountains and beyond, but towards the south a veil covered the lands beyond the horizon, reaching into the skies and behind the translucent veil of bluish tint huge dark clouds brewed, thick tendrils of darkness with flickering red light within it stretching towards the ground in a fit of fury, striking the ground mercilessly with an insane madness.

"The Swamps," Ferhia wanted to speak, but could simply inhale deeply, aghast. It was total madness, how something so powerful with the capability of mass destruction could even exist in the world as she knew it, and if the veil had not withheld their power she would have been ripped to shreds.

"Finally, we have arrived," Kilfer muttered into the cold wind as they descended to the ground. Snow covered the land and there was no sight of any living being other than them until they saw from afar, but very dimly a dim greenish hue lit up the cold white background ever so slightly.

"What is that?" Ferhia squinted into the distance, and they trudged towards it through the thick snow-smudged land. The faint glow grew brighter until faint shapes of huts could be barely visible, the top of the huts topped with chunks of snow.

"Illusions," Kilfer whispered into her ears, "There are many illusions here if you were to notice. The snow is false."

Then Ferhia started to realize it was not at all cold, but she imagined the cold herself. Kilfer squeezed her hand tight, then released it and suddenly the world around her changed, and what was there was simply trees and meadows but they were not as green as those they saw in the forest, and grayish patches of mud lay on the ground. Then they paused. The glowing light was still there -- and it was not an illusion or the work of someone, and also it was not a single cottage or hut, but an entire village.

Both of them stood dumbfounded, that an entire village could reside in such a spot where the first thing its inhabitants see in the morning is not the sunrise, nor do they hear the chimes of sweet bells, but a huge looming storm with winds hurling sand and trees from the ground with a vengeance.

"This is so clear it can't be an illusion, and the magic of the dark powers within do not extend to this place," Kilfer glanced at Ferhia with uncertainty, "How is it even possible for this to happen?"

"Intruderssss!" A shrill voice yelled from within the village walls, and the next thing they knew a volley of arrows shot out from within, short but deadly and with direct precision, but Kilfer stopped them midair and sent them spiraling back.

Ferhia glanced at Kilfer, but he simply gave a not-so-reas-suring grin. He beckoned for her to hide behind a tree, which tree bark was so huge that at least three grown men could hide behind it.

"Magic-wielders, show yourselves!" A voice rang out, this time the voice seemed strong and firm, but Kilfer placed a hand on his lips.

"Let me give you one last chance. Show yourselves!"

Kilfer broke a low tree branch from the top and spun right, out from his hiding spot, "Fine, if you insist."

The noises behind the wall halted abruptly, and one by one tiny faces popped up from behind, and then the whispering continued. From behind the tree, Ferhia noticed the tree branch Kilfer held glowing with magic, yet Kilfer pretended nothing happened and strode slowly forward.

The gate slowly moved, metal grinding against metal as it did so, and even before the gates opened fully Kilfer could see a short being barely half the height of himself, and on his hand, there was a yellowish glow of a staff...

Then the little being struck with a deadly blow, the magic sizzling its way through the thin air and Kilfer barely dodged it. He threw the branch at the figure, but it dodged nimbly away, and it was then Kilfer finally saw how the figure looked like.

Half as tall as Kilfer, his seemingly dis-proportionate beard for his height reached down, brushing down on the floor with each step he took.

"A human, with magic," The dwarf spoke, as chilling as ice, "What do you even seek here?"

"The Swamps is all we need. Show us the way there safely, and you shall not be tormented by this 'human with magic'," Kilfer raised an eyebrow.

"Then what do you need to go there? There..." The dwarf paused, and he noticed that he was staring straight at Kilfer, studying him carefully and exploring every thought in his mind.

"I...see," After a long time, the dwarf spoke, choosing his words carefully, "You are the human leader of the Pack, I see. Your visions, I see. Um, let me notify the others, things are changing, the darkness is getting powerful... and I see you brought a friend, the one who is the root of all the troub..." The dwarf fell silent and seemed to know about all his thoughts and secrets he was trying his best to hide. Ferhia emerged from behind the tree, and the dwarf turned back to the village, "Come with me, I need to talk to both of you, and how much you know about this."

Glancing at the dwarf as he tottered clumsily back, Ferhia was filled with uncertainty whether she should follow, but as Kilfer followed she knew that she had too.

***

There were hundreds of many little beings which Kilfer called them 'dwarfs', and she stood twice the height above most them. The dwarf brought them to a little shed where both of them could barely fit their bodies into, but inside it was larger than it seemed. A long flight of stairs led down to a huge hall under the ground, a globe of white mist hovered in the middle, steaming with energy.

"Here is where the globe protects us from the darkness in the Swamps, the veil of protection is held by this, and for ages, it has brought safety and prosperity to us, and to your kind as well," The dwarf spoke, "But now it seems that the Pack has perished--"

"How did you know?" Kilfer cut him off sharply.

"I can read your mind, young Kilfer. I even know your name!" The dwarf chuckled, "And coming back, the Pack is one of the roots of magic, and since they have died, perished from this world, this is a sign that the darkness is rising again, we have to notify all the masters around the world, and--"

"So would you show us the way to the Swamps so that we can revive the pack and seek revenge on those that killed my family?" Kilfer asked impatiently, cutting him off again.

"Ho! Nononono, young Kilfer. Things are not as easy as they seem. You can go into the marshes, but there is no easy way in, every way, you would encounter huge man-eating spiders and beasts. And even if you happen to get through to face your enemy, your experience and magic -- even if you could will the forces of nature -- would be too puny to even harm your foe by the slightest bit. But if you still want to leave, I shall not stop you. My last advice for you is that: Do not enter the Swamps, it only would mean certain death for you and your friend, and perhaps, if the effect of the curse of your friend is unlocked and the veil is gone, we would all perish. Not only you but me, the fellow people of your kind, cities, villages, forests, grasslands and all that is there. It would be all gone."

No one spoke as the dwarf studied Ferhia and Kilfer with his old, experienced eyes. "We will go, and nothing is stopping us," Kilfer shook his head with determination.

"Then maybe in the near future, you might be the cause of the destruction of this world, young Kilfer. The night should be coming, I am lethargic, you can stay here for the night as there are man-eating beings outside of our walls, and you are free to leave anytime after dawn," The dwarf hobbled up the stairs, and then Kilfer and Ferhia was left in the hall. Silence washed over them as they glanced at each other, no one uttering a word.

Chapter 12

The Alpha lay on a rock, its eyes shut tight, seemingly in a deep sleep if there was not a deep red bloodied stain on its body. The other wolves lay, partially covered in the deep snow, and the scene drew closer.

There was a twitch, suddenly on its snout. The view paused, before drawing closer till it was so close it was right beside the Alpha's eyes.

Then it opened.

The Alpha's eyes flickered open. But its eyes flared with savageness, red and menacing and bloodthirsty like a wolf born to kill. The wolf the Alpha once was was long gone, now he could feel the indomitable spirit for revenge and the will to slaughter.

***

Kilfer woke.

The dream was so surreal, and he woke in gasps of shock, and slowly he surveyed the surroundings. It was still the silence of the night, accompanied by the soft night breeze.

Ferhia was still asleep, but Kilfer just could not sleep, as the reddish glow of the Alpha's eyes in his dream still scorched his mind.

"Young Kilfer," A voice whispered from behind him, he turned and there the old dwarf stood.

"Oh hi," Kilfer jumped but pretended nothing happened.

"Let us talk," The dwarf hobbled up the steps, and Kilfer followed suit. Outside, the wind was not just a silent wisp, but a raging gust that whipped across Kilfer and the dwarf's cheeks continuously. The dwarf continued with Kilfer trailing behind until they finally entered a hut that Kilfer barely managed to fit through. It was a simple single-storeyed structure and in the interior is a wooden floor with a rectangular table and four chairs, all looking so simple in design.

"Come, have a seat," The dwarf ushered him to the table and they sat, while the dwarf continued, "Bronswig is my name, sorry that we did not have a good introduction to each other previously. But I have vision about the Pack--"

"I have a vision too," Kilfer cut him off yet again, "About the Pack. About the Alpha."

"What dream, you speak first, young Kilfer."

"The Alpha has awakened, its blood-red eyes. The eyes of a killer seemed so surreal, I have a bad feeling..." Kilfer's voice trailed away.

"I see. I have the same vision. This is my final warning. When you step within the Swamps, beware your family, for the spirit of the Pack might have been used by the evil forces against... you. Beware, young Kilfer. Beware," Bronswig leapt down from the chair and tottered towards the window, where the first light emnated from the east, "As the five hundredth leader of the dwarf race, I never thought the darkness would rise during my time. But now times are changing. No matter how powerful we are, fate still goes its path and there is nothing we can do to stop it."

Bronswig turned back to Kilfer, "But I hope fate would be kind to us, and I am sure of that."

***

As day came Kilfer and Ferhia left, and Bronswig showed them the shortest route to the Swamps but still full of dangerous traps from savage beings that stalk the Swamps.

They neared the veil to the Swamps by midday, and they felt a tugging sensation towards the Swamps, something they could not see, perchance an echo in their minds, so faint but powerful, dragging them towards the Swamps.

"You feel it?" Ferhia frowned, thrusting her gaze upwards where the veil extended upwards into the cloud, "It seems like something is calling to us..."

She paused when Kilfer placed a finger on his lips, and they halted. There was silence all around them -- until she heard it, a whistle of a simple tune emnating from the bushes in front. Silently, Kilfer crept towards the direction of the music, while Ferhia crept stealthily behind.

The bushes led to a grass patch, separated by the veil, the misty veil blurred what was on the other side, but they could still make out the silhouette of a woman dressed in old fabric playing a flute. Ferhia glanced at Kilfer, who swallowed anxiously. They did not know who was that, but the fact that she is on the other end of the veil (which, in short, meant that she is in the boundaries of the Swamps) meant that she is not a normal human as they were.

Between the duo and the woman was simply a few metres, but between them was the veil, the separation between living beings and the dark forces. The tension swelled to a deafening crescendo and they did not move, but instead the woman stopped mid-note, and placed her flute on the stone she sat on, and turned.

Time was stagnant to Ferhia for a moment until she faced them. Her features were just like the normal woman they saw, but something seemed so different about her, they did not know. Something that was so subduing that made Kilfer want to walk past the veil towards her. Kilfer frowned, and turned towards Ferhia. She seemed to have lost her consciences, blindly staring forward, taking slow, shaky steps forward lije being controlled.

Kilfer turned back. The woman smiled, her lips curling upwards slightly. "Come, come to me," The woman's voice echoed, "Come and I shall give you what you want. Parents, right? You do want parents, yes? Then come forth, your parents are here waiting for you."

"Stop!" Kilfer let out a burst of magic that sizzled through the veil to the woman, and she was thrown back. For a moment, her face changed into a four fanged, ten eyed monster with limbs as long as ten feet with spines from its back that stretched out from its bony body at grotesque angles, and Ferhia finally jolted back, bewildered.

"Who are you?" Kilfer took a step back as the devilish creature inched forward.

"You need not know, mere mortal," It placed a bony palm on the veil, "But halt. How do you have magic with your blood? What do you seek? Monies? Power? Glory? I have them all." It studied Kilfer for a moment, before grinning, its bony cheeks flicked upward, "Or the Pack, alive?"

That caught both Kilfer and Ferhia by shock, and Kilfer unleashed a pounding blow of magic directly slamming into the creature right through the veil. The creature tried to ise its own magic, but no matter how hard it tried no magic could reach Kilfer.

Silently, it bounded back, deep into the Swamps and Kilfer knelt on the muddy soil, his face expressionless. Or the pack, alive? The words revolved in his mind, the temptation he tried so hard to forget but just could not.

"Kilfer," Ferhia spoke beside him, "Don't listen to it, the Pack is..."

"No, you don't understand," Ferhia could see tears in Kilfer's eyes, no matter how hard he tried to conceal it, "I had a dream, so surreal. That the Alpha is coming for me. It's red eyes of an assasin... I can even visualize it now..."

Kilfer's voice trailed away, and Ferhia let out a deep sigh, not because of the dream or the creature, but because of Kilfer. She loved him as a brother, even though they did not speak to each other often she still could not bear to see his heart punctured with sorrow and grief.

"Let's go," Kilfer finally stood up, "If the Alpha wants to kill me, or is manipulated to kill me or anything, let it be the case. I shall face anything to avenge the Pack."

***

They ventured through the veil, which was thicker than they expected, and as soon as they passed it a pungent smell took over their senses, those of rotting meat and flesh while everything was in a chaos, winds threatened to hurl them into the air and ripped into shreds, and bats and remnants of trees (which mostly were left with tree barks and probably one or two brown leaves) filled the place, the ground trembled and shook as if it were alive. Ferhia did not know how Kilfer thought, but to himself this should be the exact resemblance of hell.

They staggered fowards, holding hands and once in a while when Kilfer or Ferhia peered up to the skies filled with thick, dark skies that seemed to resemble the hate and menace in around them. The clouds took form of huge faces, their empty eye sockets filled with greenish light and the clouds that took on those phantom-like faces morphed around each other, sometimes forming huge faces and dissipating into several smaller ones.

"Ferhia, greetings," A voice whispered in Ferhia's ears. Ferhia jumped and turned, but there was no one besides the brown sand and gravel blown around them.

'Who are you?' Ferhia thought in her mind, trying to communicate with the voice.

"You need not know for now. But I mean no harm... as long as you comply."

'Comply? To what?" Ferhia frowned.

"Just do as I say, I own the Swamps. Your brother wants the Pack back alive and you want your parents? Yes, they are with me. However before you meet them you must follow what I say. Take ten steps to the right, and close your eyes."

Ferhia decided not to reply, aware that the Swamps was a place that they might die anytime. She squeezed Kilfer's hand and he turned towards her.

"Come," Ferhia yelled over the roaring of the wind, and Kilfer seemed bewildered but followed her. Together, they took the ten steps and closed their eyes, suddenly Ferhia could not feel the wind, instead it was exchanged by numbness, cold, she felt it.

"Open your eyes," The voice echoed in her mind. Ferhia did so, and the wind was totally gone, the dark ferocious clouds and the veil was gone, now all the sounds was only replaced by the soft clang of glass on glass, the sound was like diamond -- so transparent, so serene -- yet for some reason seemed dangerous.

Kilfer was nowhere to be seen, but she was wary about the place, all the stone statues around the side of the hall made her feel uneasy. Then from the corner of her eyes a statue moved. She swivelled her gaze to the statue, and its limbs started moving, and as it did so the ground beneath her split open and she leapt back in shock. From beneath, two stone sarcophagus raised up, each one carved as a wolf's face on the bottom face of each sarcophagus, and at the top it was a face, one of a man and one of a woman.

"Greetings, Ferhia. And welcome!" From within the wall a voice echoed, and a part of the wall tumbled down, revealing a throne made of glass, and on top was someone, yet everytime she brought her eyes to meet it her eyes simply would not obey her.

"The spirits of your parents are within -- I have trapped them, and they can return to their mortal bodies, if you would not try to escape," The figure on the throne seemed to be mocking her, "And by the way, call me the Ghost, if that may please you."

Ferhia did not want to speak. The darkness was right in front of her, but she could not kill it, but it was just in front of him. Only if she could...

"Before I let you return to your parents, let me just show you... something interesting," Within the low monotonous voice of the Ghost there was a tint of humor. A vision spread across her pupils, and what appeared first is Kilfer lying, and the vision morphed into the Alpha, red-eyed, and Kilfer stood, cornered on a wall.

"Look, they are having so much fun," A voice whispered in her head. On the screen, the Alpha cornered Kilfer on a wall. The wolf's eyes were deep red, and Ferhia could see within. The hatred, the bitterness and the wanting for revenge. The canine inched closer, snarling, and leapt forward.

Ferhia did not dare to open her eyes, but there was warm, thick fluid running down her face. She opened her eyes, the Alpha was already on Kilfer. On her face was the blood of her brother. The leader of the pack. Kilfer.

The wolf turned, its blood red eyes staring into her. She felt small, weak, and could be gnarled to pieces between the wolves' teeth. "Yes, my dear," The voice spoke, this time even more menacing, "Slaughter her."

Then, the last vision she saw was the canine's razor teeth clamping down on her, and the next thing was darkness.

It was her own dream barely a few days ago, Ferhia realised that. "Let him die," The Ghost's voice echoed, then followed by a mirth of laughter, and the scene turned back to Kilfer on the bed, not showing a sign of pain but blood was seeping out of his tunic.

Save him. A voice sounded in her head, willing her to rush forward and wake Kilfer out of the horrendous, demonic dream that was plaguing him and stealing his life force away.

Ferhia took a step towards Kilfer.

"Don't do anything!" The Ghost's voice echoed in her mind, "Or your parents' soul shall not return once I let them out of the sarcophagus!"

Ferhia paused, but after a second sprinted towards her brother lying on the floor.

"Stop! NOW!" The Ghost's voice sounded, this time louder but Ferhia continued. The view of Kilfer was escaping from her vision, but she knew that she could make it.

Three more steps.

Two more.

One more...

Then she pushed Kilfer, just as the view receded totally from her view.

Ferhia woke, and at the same time she saw the Ghost, and could even sense its hatred and vengeance.

"You wanted to kill my brother!" Ferhia yelled, but the Ghost paid her no heed.

"This is your last chance," Ferhia felt the temperature in the hall soaring, and the Ghost's voice was filled with anger, "Give me your blood, or I will achieve it by force."

"No," Ferhia heard herself say.

Chapter 13

Kilfer woke.

Something felt wrong in his blood, he felt it. Someone was in trouble.

Ever since he woke up from the dream, he felt it. Kilfer closed his eyes for a moment, felt where the distress was and hurried through the only opening. Something that was powerful was near, he felt it but ignored the brewing sensation he might be trampling onto something dangerous.

Finally, he hurried out, where the tunnel opened to an entire hall, stone statues covered the sides of the hall and in the middle dark tendrils of magic was reaching onto someone, a girl with the tattered white tunic, and blood seeped out onto the ground.

Atop the throne that dwarfed all in the hall a dark figure sat, and he stared straight at its face, right within the black mists that shrouded its face, and finally saw its face, but it was a myriad of faces, turning from Ferhia's to the Alpha's to his own.

"Mere mortal," Its tone was calm but venomous, "You can't see my true countenance, stop your futile attempts, the curse has finally gone its course in my favor, I have already consumed the blood of the cursed, and finally the veil can be broken by me! Face your fate, the Pack can never be resurrected, only I can allow their resurrection -- against you."

The Ghost raised up above its throne, a huge gust of wind suddenly swirling around the hall, and Kilfer saw Ferhia from the corner of his eyes Kilfer saw Ferhia's limp body precariously lying near the throne where the dark magic throbbed.

"Ferhia!" He yelled, trying to use his magic to will Ferhia's body to her, but the wind was too powerful that even he struggled hard to keep himself on the ground.

"Farewell, and we shall never meet," That was the last word Kilfer heard before everything disappeared.

Silence.

Kilfer was crouched in a corner, the voice of the Ghost still imprinted in his mind. The Ghost. He knew that name from the prophecy, bringer of death and destruction. He had vowed to avenge the Pack and kill whoever stood against him and find Ferhia's parents, but when she really stood before the Ghost he could do nothing, powerless and weak.

But now, Ferhia was the only one in the entire realm that he could care for, and the only one who would care for him. He staggered towards her and felt within her inner self. She was dead -- at least her mortal self was dead, but he could feel the soul of Ferhia and that meant that she could still be brought back to life.

'Only if there was one powerful enough. Only if...' Kilfer paused in his thoughts, remembering something.

"Mizervon, the first human leader of the Pack," Kilfer spoke out loud. Even though those that said Mizervon was still alive somewhere were simply rumors, he knew he had to try to find him, probably the old dwarf Mizervon knows something.

He stood, and felt the opening from the hall, and left using his magic to carry Ferhia out, with that tiny glimmer of a chance that Mizervon might be on the map of the realm somewhere, and he is powerful enough to face The Ghost and all the other madness he brought with him...

Chapter 14

His rushed footsteps was heavy on the stone floor, his sister's weight on his back.

Thirty steps, he could see the opening.

Twenty steps... ten steps...

Kilfer burst out of the darkness, watching the rolling storms of darkness, the stench of rotting flesh and the feel of pure evil made him halt his breathing for a moment, and within the darkness he could seem to catch a glimpse of the darkest darkness within, a hulking figure growing more powerful within the minute.

As the dark storms drew closer, wiping plants and animals from the land and birds from the skies Kilfer spotted a deer, its ears perked up and staring intently at the storms.

Kilfer placed a hand on the animal's back and whispered to it, "Come, bring me to Bronswig."

He had a feeling the little dwarf knew something about Mizervon, and when the deer glanced at him sceptically he showed it the marking he had of his palm -- that of a wolf with a diamond on the top. From a million miles from the veil, humans, animals and spirits knew it was the sigil of a member of the Pack, as although the Pack was so secluded it was so powerful in magic that the those who bore the sigil were both feared and hated, and Kilfer would usually keep the sigil to himself. The deer paused for a moment and bowed low for him to ride.

The deer raced across the lands, the stench of the Swamps lagging behind them and finally, Kilfer could catch a whiff of the fresh air -- but he knew it would not be long until these lands were usurped by the darkness.

Finally, from afar the little buildings approached him and as soon as he reached the village he leapt off the deer, nearly tripping by the weight of Ferhia above him.

"I guessed as much," Bronswig stood in front of him, right after he regained his balance."The darkness..."

"Yes, I know of it all, the darkness, our greatest nightmare had finally risen... again," Bronswig glanced beyond him to the horizons, where the darkness is still brewing, "There is now none but a choice, and I am sure you know of it. Mizervon."

"Wait, do you mean..." A spark of hope appeared on Kilfer's countenance.

"Yes, the chance of really getting to him is really minute, but I am sure that I kept a map leading to the first leader of the Pack, say no more and follow me," Bronswig ran, seeming quite comical with the short legs and Kilfer followed behind, saying much less nothing.

They went into a building which, Kilfer was quite perplexed, that there were totally no windows, but the architecture within was even more perplexing, the walls were made of tiny moving orbs, and so were the tables and chairs and every other thing within as if it were controlled by a mystical force.

"Here," Bronswig picked up a slip of paper, withered and yellowed throughout the years, only remaining a few rough scribbles on the paper, "This would take you to the residence of Mizervon, I will try to hold the darkness for as long as I can, but be quick."

"Master Bronswig!" The door blasted open and a dwarf twice the height of Bronswig himself (which was considered exceptionally tall for a dwarf and Kilfer already noticed him from his first visit to the village) ran towards him, panting, "The darkness is arriving, we must be quick!"

"Not that I have to be reminded, Wyle," Bronswig grumbled, "I will be there soon, just leave with the rest!"As the dwarf Wyle slipped out of the door Bronswig turned back to Kilfer, and Kilfer could see the sadness in Bronswig's aged eyes and felt his own feeling of the reluctance to part with this village. Bronswig passed a box to him and placed Ferhia within, and Ferhia shrank to a seventh of her original size. "Hope that helps," Bronswig mumbled and sealed the lid tight, "Go, now and waste time no more."Kilfer was about to leave when

Bronswig spoke behind him, "If you happen to lose your way, always remember -- stay with what you trust most and let it guide you."

Kilfer paused at the doorway, but decided to continue and did not turn back

***

Kilfer rode the deer across the grasslands, the box that held Ferhia's mortal self and spirit clamped tightly between his hands, and glanced behind. The village seemed to get smaller with every gallop, as the deer brought him further away, but the wall of darkness seemed to get even closer and the storms, like an incoming wave swept everything in its path into the devastating maelstrom within.

"Ferhia," Kilfer placed the box close to his ears, and spoke into the tiny opening, hoping for perchance a soft breath, "Can... can you hear me?"

There was no reply, and Kilfer waited, feeling the rhythmic rocking of the deer. She could hear me, Kilfer knew, clearly feeling his sister's presence in the box, but she simply declined to reply. Yet before Kilfer could even continue, he felt a squeezing sensation in his heart, the painful feeling of the loss of someone, and he brought the horse to a halt, placing a hand on his chest. His heart was beating fast, and he turned -- there a shield so mighty held the waves darkness like a final rock preventing the ocean from destroying all that remains of a beautiful land.Bronswig's lifeforce. Kilfer was taken aback. No magician could weave such a powerful magic except for using his or her own lifeforce, which also meant the Spirit of a man destroyed utterly, and the massive pain to do it... Kilfer could not bear to think further, even the thoughts hurt him.

He closed his eyes and let the horse carry himself away, silent tears, hot and filled with grief streaked down his countenance, mixing with the anger and sadness and the wanting to stay and destroy the darkness to seek revenge for all including Ferhia and Bronswig, but yet the futility in those thoughts drove him forward and he could not let all the sacrifices go to naught.

He had to be quick.

Chapter 15

Kilfer enjoyed the rhythmic rocking of the deer as it bounded seemingly effortlessly across vast distances, watching the green plants and other animals and flowers and bees go by. In fact, Kilfer just loved it, the feeling made him forget everything, all the pains and hard times he went through, it all seemed far from him now.

He glanced at the map finally, after a long time he could not already remember the time that he realised it was just time to enter the forest on the right. They bounded within and the sunlight, wind and comfort all disappeared for just that split second of change when the damp cold feeling took hold, and for once or twice water splattered onto him and he did not do more than wipe it on his already stained tunic.

Nothing seemed to appear within his vision and it seemed just a short trail into the forest on the map, and beyond it the ink seemed worn off, surrendering to time. Finally, the deer ground to a halt and Kilfer immediately saw why. Trails of water was flowing on the stone ground full of algae and from a distance the loud gurgling of water could be heard, only muffled by a clump of bushes that stood between Kilfer and the water source.

Silently, Kilfer leapt off the deer's back and found his way across the thicket, and what he saw disappointed him a little -- he expected a huge waterfall with Mizervon on the top with an entire marble statue carved in his favour, but it was simply a moss covered wall that the water spilled down from and the space where it fell was only a small stream, too small to even be called a river.

He turned back to the deer behind the thicket and motioned for it to follow and it did, ears perked up instinctively for any sound and dark eyes gleaming like an eclipse to catch any movement. They emerged once again, Kilfer grabbing a fruit and tossing it into his mouth, and once the deer caught sight of the water it made a sound that seemed sort of a whine, as if it caught sight of something so horrendous, and when Kilfer glanced suspiciously at the animal it padded forward and placed a hoof into the water but Kilfer, wary of what could happen. Then, unexpectedly with a fluid motion the deer leapt right into the water.

Then the deer sank, slowly, smoothly, without a tint of struggle and the deer glanced at Kilfer for the last moment before its ears disappeared underwater.

Kilfer was too stunned to react, although he could control water that was something totally new to him, and he took a few steps forward until he wad directly in front of the water. It seemed calm and when Kilfer glanced down, peering into the water what appeared was simply his own reflection, like how water seemed like. But once Kilfer placed a finger into the water it felt totally different from water, and he leapt into the water, letting the soft feeling of the water wash over him slowly, he did not feel uncomfortable but simply closed his eyes and let himself submerge, and did not breathe...

Kilfer opened his eyes. He felt the cold feeling of stone on his back, and sat up. There was only dim light piecing through the ceiling, and the deer was missing, only leaving the box that held Ferhia which lay beside him. He glanced around, but besides the overwhelming darkness there was nothing, yet he felt relieved. This was calm darkness, silent yet not foreboding, the darkness that allowed the light to flourish within it, the darkness that gave serenity but not destruction.

Kilfer took a step forward. He had clearly remembered the map stopped there and he did not remember seeing anything after that, and what could happen in the pitch darkness was still unknown. Kilfer took another step, and another, but with every step he took there was a growing and gnawing sensation that something in the darkness knows of his presence, and is watching his every movement, but pretended not to notice.

Kilfer counted the steps until ten, and from the darkness faint smears of light danced around in his vision, and he squinted forward.

"Kilfer," A voice echoed simply like the wind whistling across his ears, but it never escaped his ears and he yelled into the darkness, "Who goes there?"

Something smooth and light sweeped across his hands and he yelped, jumping and turned, but there a figure stood, murmuring verses he could not comprehend, and all of a sudden he felt dizzy, the figure in front of him spreading into six beings in front of him as his vision blurred.

When the dizziness stopped the darkness disappeared, and there was a single girl there, and she beckoned him to follow her, "Come."

Kilfer did not know why he followed her and felt no fear at all. All that had happened since he leapt down from the waterfall happened so quickly and now he did not even know what could happen next, and did not know where he was going, then the girl paused in front abruptly, "Here, if there was an abominable darkness consuming it all in this room and you only had two choices to escape, which would you choose?"

Kilfer followed her gaze to two windows, one that was filled with darkness and the other filled with light."The darkness consumes light. Light is its prey, and if the light was there the darkness would have foraged for light within the window of light." Kilfer spoke aloud, remembering Bronswig's last words to him, "If you happen to lose your way, always remember -- stay with what you trust most and let it guide you."

"But it I enter the window of darkness," Kilfer thought of the similarity of his predicament to the window of darkness, where he was stranded within, trying to seek light so powerful that could resist the darkness, "There might be just that tiny speck of light far within the hopeless darkness that is so mighty that could resist all the demonic torture of the darkness, and I can use it, against all evil. I shall enter the window of darkness then."

"Off you go then," The girl raised a hand and Kilfer suddenly felt light, and in his vision he was not touching the ground but levitating, the window of darkness expanded larger and larger until it spread over his vision.

And swallowed Kilfer whole.

Chapter 16

Kilfer had a bad dream.

He dreamt of thousands of ants, black and huge with an unstoppable craving for fresh meat and blood. They were tearing apart his flesh, burrowing deep into his skin and bringing out a throbbing red lump of flesh that he realised what it was. His heart.

He saw it with his own eyes, yet felt no pain except for the numbness that clung to his body. He lay there limp, simply watching the gruesome procession of the ants eating him and burrowing holes on his skin silently. Motionlessly.

Then he woke.

Kilfer was in a different place, the darkness was gone, and so were the ants and the waterfall and the windows and the veil and everything that he knew of, leaving him and the box the held Ferhia beside him. Thick long strands of grass filled the entire span of land until the horizon from where he could see, but when he turned to the other side there was simply mountains. He was lost, he did not know where he came to, and where he should continue on, and when he glanced at the map there was not a single mark like it was simply a blank piece of paper.

Kilfer could simply sigh as he bent down to retrieve the box. It was so light it seemed that Ferhia had simply the weight of a pound of lead, silent, hard and unmoving. He knew simply waiting would not help, and he must go forward, for wasting more time might mean the darkness consuming all he knew and treasured, including him and Ferhia.

"If you happen to lose your way, always remember -- stay with what you trust most and let it guide you," Bronswig's words echoed in his mind. Kilfer paused, glancing around and saw nothing except for a river, calm and silent, only a slight gurgling sound. Following the water, it extended northwards, up to the mountains where the mist and freezing temperatures lay.

The river. Kilfer remembered how he always found the way back to the Lair when he is lost on the mountain during the days when the Pack was still alive, and he had always trusted the river, the sounds of the water soothed him and the soft touch of the water made him love water more than anything else within all the magic that he could control.

Glancing down into the river water he pulled deep into the water, concentrating deep within every molecule and willing it towards him. They followed and bit by bit, water rose from the river until it seemed a hulking azure figure, and Kilfer leapt onto it, driving the water he gathered forwards, sweeping the grass with freshly gathered water and driving the water back into the river with a splash.

Kilfer loved the water, and once he found how to use water with his powers barely a few days ago he loved the sensation, the fluidity of the liquid that he concentrated within him, and the beauty that his powers gave it, to make it alive.

The water carried him forwards, the view of the mountains getting larger, closer and the northern winds blew gusts of cool wind towards him and he welcomed it, it was so long since he felt the wind this refreshing to him.

He glanced back to the box, he remembered how he found Ferhia, her sister. She never knew of a vision Kilfer had, that on the day he turned five a cursed girl shall be born, and she is Kilfer's only bloodline. No one, not even the Pack or Ferhia knew but they were connected, Kilfer and Ferhia, as brothers and sisters and how he took pains to bring Ferhia into the Pack against the wolves' will. Five years ago before Ferhia was born, it was him who was thrown out of the village because of the curse. He also had the curse, and was of the same parentage as Ferhia. And it was also the Pack that saved him from the cold, silent night the night he was thrown out of the village.

Kilfer sighed. If he did not bring Ferhia into the Pack he would still be living joyously with the Pack and the Alpha and the curse would not have gone its course... but Ferhia was family.

Kilfer stood, and willed it to move even faster, rushing through the river and for every second picking up even more speed, until he reached the mountain did he stop and leap down to the riverbank. Glancing up, the gentle hill steeped up, leaving barely a ledge for him to step on, and it extended long into the mist, and nothing could be seen beyond. He could not change the shape of mountains with his current wizardry skills, and could simply continue with this treacherous journey, even if it might mean certain death.

Muttering silent verses of prayers Kilfer took his first steps up, the hill seemed easy enough, just a gentle slope upwards but soon it narrowed further until there was only room for a single foot at a time to move across the ledge. Beneath, the cliff emptied to nothingness and he shut his eyes tight and groped for something on the cliff face that he could grope on, and only found a smooth cliff face, and he inhaled, clutching the box tighter, and felt that its weight seemed to increase, then a slight cold breeze caressed his face, then he grabbed hold of the wind with his magic, and leapt onto the breeze an unseen force that rippled across the air and Kilfer tried hard to keep himself aloft with only the breeze, but as he entered the mists huge winds blew him back towards the ledge, knocking him off course and he held onto the ledge with a hand and the box on another.

"Ferhia," Kilfer reached deep into the spirit within the box and pleaded as the last ounce of strength slipped beyond his grasp and he was about to fall towards what lay beneath the mountains, "Save me."

Yet, there was still no reply, a dead box with a spirit that could not speak within, Kilfer felt hate within him. He wanted to simply hurl the box to the valley below and get to safety, but he just could not. She was his sister and he must not let go.

Then, Kilfer heard the unmistakable sound of water echoing from within the mist. The sounds of a waterfall, and when he extended his feel of magic towards the mist an entire waterfall appeared in his vision, a wall of water extending in a fluid, graceful movement down towards the valley below. He grasped the water with an unseen force and released his hand on the ledge. For a moment he was in the middle of the mist, and he thought he was falling for a split second until he tugged hard onto the water of the waterfall did he get raised through the air, and finally, when he burst out of the mist the entire waterfall appeared before his eyes. The waterfall was gargantuan, far larger than the waterfall he felt using his magic. Behind the cliff, there was simply small slopes adorned with grass and oak trees and insects and animals that seemed to make this mountain a stark contrast to the other stony, cold mountains and it seemed to be a land of its own.

Kilfer landed on the grass and turned back to catch a view of the surrounding mountains, and all he saw were chunks of white snow draped across the cold scenery, lifeless. He turned back and found that the river flowed upstream, and seemed to be showing him to somewhere. Grabbing the box he left, following the stream of water closely, and stopped when the water receded underground into a hole, and Kilfer sighed. He had trusted the river and came so long to find nothing. Perhaps, Mizervon had perished like all the other mortal souls over the generations, and he sat on the ground, his mind was blank, and then he caught the smell of cinnamon bread, he had only tasted them once, and he simply loved the smell. Following the fragrance, Kilfer went up a small hill and on top, he saw smoke, buildings and an entire village atop a pasture, and the smell of cinnamon was even stronger, revitalizing his senses. It was simply a short walk from the hill to the village, but once Kilfer reached the village he noticed something that was totally strange -- for all the houses and stalls all were perfectly set up, the fruits and fish were fresh, and so were the many loaves of cinnamon bread freshly baked and all was normal, except that it was totally empty, with no hint of any human presence.

Kilfer took every step with caution as his experiences told him that anything could happen, and every step brought him closer to the cinnamon bread, and that sharp twitch in his stomach reminded him how long he had not had a proper meal. He reached out for the bread, and just at the moment he spotted a movement and swiveled around, and caught sight of a small boy peeking out from behind a wall.

"Wait... who are you?" The boy scowled, then seemed to realize something, "You're a traveler, aren't you? Quick, the dark horde is coming, let me bring you to the hideout."

Kilfer did not know what to say, but simply nodded, and went with the boy warily. He was the first living person Kilfer saw since he came to this place, and Kilfer thought that he might know something about the whereabouts of Mizervon. They walked through small streets and alleyways, and on one he could vaguely see a name scrawled on the wall, hidden so well yet unable to escape from Kilfer's eyes, 'The Hideout'.

"Here," The boy paused in front of him, "Get in, its safe." Kilfer peered to where the boy was jabbing at and saw a trapdoor the same color of the ground that swung out to reveal a hole small enough for a fully grown man to pass through.

"Where is this place?" Kilfer spoke for the first time, and the boy turned, "Wait, your accent does not seem familiar, where do you come from?"

"The mainland, I guess," Kilfer remembered how someone told him that the land they came from was the 'mainland', largest in all the worlds and realms that had ever been discovered.

"I see," The boy frowned, "That means you really are a traveler from such a distant place, come in."They descended into darkness and finally reached a room, stuffy and uncomfortably warm but there were many people, young and old huddled inside.

"What..." Kilfer uttered a word before the boy turned to Kilfer, "Oh, sorry for not introducing ourselves, I am Mirdaff and here not many travelers come, so everyone is treasured here. By the way, this is our grand leader Otnoybsk."

Otnoybsk, Kilfer thought, what a weird name. Kilfer took a step forward to greet Otnoybsk he expected a wizened old man in long golden robes but instead, it was a young man, but his face seemed fearful, and all the villagers appeared to be anxious too.

"Welcome, young traveler," He spoke half-heartedly, and Kilfer replied, "Kilfer is my name, and I am no traveler but simply seek something."

"And that is..."

"The whereabouts of Mizervon," Kilfer decided to reveal and trust the villagers for they might not know who Mizervon even is and they were the only ones he could trust now. No one spoke for a moment, but Kilfer noticed that the atmosphere started to turn uneasy, and Otnoybsk shook his head slowly, "No, the road from here is treacherous, most people whom we have met over the years have gone... and never came back."

"But I will, and we are all in great danger if you would not believe, that the veil is broken and the darkness is coming anytime soon. We need Mizervon," Kilfer glanced at them, and realized how warm it was in the room, and frowned, "But wait, why do we need to hide here? It is really warm."

"The dark horde is coming, we saw them from afar, it is lucky that you weren't caught by them on your way here," Mirdaff answered, "The dark horde are the savage contesters for territory, and they come every three days, and today, they will come again. They are cold-blooded, bloodthirsty and have a never diminishing instinct to kill. They are the largest threat to us, and they can't seem to die... but when they are not attacking us, they seem to be searching, foraging for something else that we do not know..."

Kilfer wanted to say something, that all the things that happened came too abrupt and a million questions still revolved within his mind, but he had to keep the thoughts to himself for a horn sounded in the distance, and without anyone telling him he knew what was about to happen: The dark horde is just at their doorsteps.

"Stay silent," Otnoybsk placed a finger on his lips and whispered, while the other fifty - or - so villagers kept totally silent within the room.

Kilfer could hear many sounds up on the ground -- porcelain bowls crashing onto the ground and hacking of walls and once or twice there was a squeal of cats being stomped on the ground to death, and they even smelt fire from where they were underground.

It all happened in a few minutes or so, and soon all the noises eroded into silence. They heard the hooves of horses riding away, the sounds of the shouts and hooves diminished until the silence was what was left, and Otnoybsk finally spoke, "They are gone, we're safe."

They climbed out of the opening to reveal the disastrous remains of the village, carcasses of stray cats on the ground and three houses were burnt to ruins as far as they could see, and all the food that was placed in the open were also not left alone, all the fruits and fish on the ground, and Kilfer turned towards Obnoybsk, "So... what now?"

"Rebuild, I believe. We have always done the same, but we can't fight back. People say that Mizervon created this horde to prevent us from ever venturing out of this mountain to search for him, and there was a prophecy that said that the day we found him, the day we would all die."

"It is untrue, a human leader of the Pack would not place such a curse on us!"

"No, young lad. You do not understand --"

"I do understand more than you do, rather than fearing that the dark horde might trample over your lands we should fear more of the darkness, they are already tearing through what is left in the living, and if we do not find Mizervon the darkness will find us, and kill us."

Otnoybsk shook his head meekly, and Kilfer could see the leader did not want to continue speaking, "I am tired, Kilfer, of speaking to you. If you are so resistant, then go you shall, but bring no ill fate to us."

Kilfer stood there while the other villagers, not knowing about their conversation left with Obnoybsk behind, and leaving a single villager behind, staring at Kilfer intently. "You're searching for Mizervon?" Mirdaff asked, and Kilfer nodded.

"Me too, actually. The other villagers also think that I am really going senile, but I do have a map at home that my father passed to me three years ago, come and I'll show you the map," Mirdaff said and disappeared behind a partially destroyed building. Kilfer followed Mirdaff across a small lane before they reached a door of a small building, the walls unfurnished for quite a long time and Mirdaff opened the door, showing a simple room within -- a bed barely large enough for Mirdaff himself, a dining spot with a meager amount of food and that was it. Around the dusty corners of the house, huge spiders and webs spread across the walls and Mirdaff's entire residence seemed so pitiful that Kilfer was astonished how Mirdaff lived in such a placed, yet said nothing.

"Here," Mirdaff seemed oblivious to the spiders and crumbling walls, unfolding a map, withered and yellow around the sides, "My father passed away two years ago, and this was the last thing he gave me. A map to Mizervon, he said. But the markings on the map are... peculiar."

Kilfer raised an eyebrow and studied the map. It was only partially drawn, and some caves and markings on the map were partially drawn, disappearing halfway, as if someone erased the markings away from the map. He could make some sense out of where they were on the map, a red blotch of ink on a mountain showing the village, but besides that, he could see nothing special. Tracing his fingers towards the North of the huge map, Kilfer spotted peculiar markings and after that, all the drawings disappeared into blank space that covered the rest of the paper. Kilfer eased back, staring at the map and wondering who would have drawn a partial map that made totally no sense to him, and he saw Mirdaff eyeing his own map he had on his hand. "What's that?" Mirdaff suddenly asked, jabbing at the map. "Ah, nothing. I thought it was a map leading to Mizervon once, but turns out it's just a blank piece of paper," Kilfer shook his head and handed him his map half-heartedly, "Here, if you really want it." Kilfer continued studying Mirdaff's map before Mirdaff showed his map in front of him, "Look, it is not blank paper! There are lines, but..." Mirdaff's voice trailed off, and Kilfer turned and was astonished to find out that there were faint traces of lines on the paper, and it certainly resembled a map rather than anything else. "But the previous time I saw it... it was empty," Kilfer turned to Mirdaff, and they stared at each other for quite a long time, but resuming their work to the map without a definite answer why the markings appeared and disappeared whenever they wanted to.

With the two maps, they found out that the two papers, if stacked at an appropriate position and with sunlight shining through, it revealed a totally different and surprisingly detailed map, showing every mountain and they managed to trace out a pathway from the rocky mountains, passing the living rocks and Lair of the Dragons to where the maps stopped far to the North before sunset.

When they finally placed their maps down for rest, Kilfer turned to Mirdaff and studied the boy once more. He was so intelligent and managed to find out secrets within the maps that Kilfer himself could not even spot, and he was a peculiar person. Ever since he was born he did not meet many people but as far as he knew Mirdaff was the only one who looked up to Mizervon's legacy and impacts to the Pack, the world and beyond by sealing up the darkness when most of the humans have already forgotten all that he did, and he was the first person Kilfer saw who wanted to search for Mizervon, and had the same goals as him. Kilfer knew that he had found a friend, a companion that would aid him throughout his journey.

"Kilfer," Mirdaff's voice interrupted his thoughts, "Dinner would be soon served, it is just tradition for all the villagers to eat together, come along!"

Surprised, Kilfer followed Mirdaff to the centre of the village, where a huge circular table was and chairs were arranged around it, and delicacies that were so expensive in the cities from Kilfer's own homeland were readily available on the table, and his eyes widened a little when he saw cinnamon bread, baskets and baskets of them placed on the table with chicken and pumpkins. They settled down for the meal and for a moment Kilfer was indulging in the meal so voraciously that he forgot what he came here for, until he realised Mirdaff who was originally beside him was gone and left a slip of paper beside him but previously he was too famished to even notice the paper, and when he read it, it was simple with only four words written on it: We need to talk.

Kilfer slipped out of all the celebration and talking around the table and all the joy and happiness and stared out into the darkness. The sun had already set, and it was difficult to see anyone with the meager amount of light present outside of the dining table. Finally, Kilfer saw Mirdaff staring at him from behind a building, and bounded over towards him.

"What's wrong?" Kilfer said when he reached Mirdaff, and the boy glanced at him, "You say the veil is broken and the darkness Mizervon sealed a thousand years ago is back as a threat again."Kilfer nodded."But how did you know, and why were you there?" Mirdaff asked, and Kilfer paused. He did not expect Mirdaff to query so much but knew that he had to reveal everything about himself.

"Look, it's complicated. I needed to save my sister who was bound to a curse and revive the pack that needed me to go beyond the veil, but instead I... I led to the darkness being freed. I am the human leader of the Pack, but instead, I failed my mission, by bringing my cursed sister into the Pack and created all of this..."

Kilfer's voice trailed into the night, and silence tossed and turned around them, and Kilfer then realized Mirdaff's charcoal colored eyes staring at him, and Mirdaff finally spoke, "You are... the human leader of the Pack?"

"Yes, and in the box that I brought with me, currently in your house, is my sister, dead but her soul can return to her original self, and I will show my vengeance to the darkness the moment I have my revenge, and that would be when I find Mizervon and the powers that shall withstand the darkness," Kilfer spoke, and with every syllable Kilfer spat hatred and he was sure Mirdaff felt the anger that the air around him was getting warmer and a warm breeze blew across their faces.

I see," Mirdaff said, and stood, "Come, let me bring you to somewhere only I know, just a short walk from here. Oh, and bring along your sister, I am sure she would be pleased to see it."

They took the box that held Ferhia and set off, the dim orange glow of light from the village slowly disappearing to a small dot until they could not even see the village lights anymore, as if the darkness took over, but they continued across the bushes until Mirdaff stopped in front of him, "Here it is."Kilfer glanced at Mirdaff, and back to where Mirdaff led him to. It was a small grass patch, and Kilfer could not see anything too special.

"Look closely," Mirdaff took a step forward into the grass, and a twinkle of light, so small and indistinct, but seemed so vibrant popped out of the grass, buzzing into the air, a small twinkle of light dancing in the air. A firefly. The sensation that the little creature gave him was so peculiar, and he had never experienced such a warm glow in his life, and he felt comfort even with this meager light, illuminating the still, cold darkness of the night.

Then, another glimmer of light buzzed to life, and another, and another, and soon the entire grass patch was not only a dull space of darkness but filled with light that echoed into Kilfer's mind as hope. Light so powerful to give all mortal beings hope, although fragile but graceful, powerful and he felt happy for the first time in his life. He sat down beside Mirdaff and watched as more and more of the little graceful beings illuminated all of the trees and bushes and flowers and all there is.

"Thank you," Kilfer whispered to Mirdaff, but got no reply. Kilfer wondered if Mirdaff did not bother to reply or that he did not hear Kilfer, but Kilfer did not bother much, but relaxed under the serenity and peace and hope that such a small act of light could nourish."Kilfer," A voice so soft echoed in his ears and he turned, there a girl stood beside him, but her body was translucent and shone a bluish glow around her, and she was smiling to him. Kilfer saw her with his own eyes, and immediately recognized who she was.

"Ferhia," Kilfer said and smiled, but with sorrow. She was so close, yet he knew that they were separated by such a vast distance, a mortal and a spirit, yet right beside each other.

"Trust yourself, my brother. You will succeed, and no matter how far we are separated, I shall aid you in all the ways I can. Be hopeful, Kilfer."

Kilfer nodded as the spirit vanished, leaving Kilfer and Mirdaff together and when Kilfer turned towards him, he noticed that Mirdaff took no notice of Ferhia's extra presence and decided not to say anything. The night still carried on, but something new sprouted within Kilfer's heart that had, a long time ago, wilted. A seedling of light. A seedling of hope...

***

A small crowd formed at the entrance of the village when the duo was about to leave the next day, and in the middle of the crowd was Otnoybsk, a wooden crate was placed below him to make him stand taller than the rest, and when the crowd caught sight of the duo, they broke into a flurry of voice until Otnoybsk calmed them down.

"You do know, that we all do not want you to leave? Especially to search for Mizervon, you do know that the entire village is here to dissuade you, but if you insist..." Otnoybsk's voice died down and turned, while two chains were brought forward, huge and rusty, the shackles clinking against each other.

"It's either going the easy way... or the hard way, and we do not want that," Otnoybsk curled his lips up, but Kilfer remained calm.

"We will still leave, no matter how you threaten us. But let me warn you, that a larger threat than you have ever seen before is arriving, and it would be soon at your doorsteps," Kilfer still stood his ground, raising his palm high and the Pack's sigil for everyone to see, "Let me pass! Or else..." An oak tree budged slowly towards them, and the villagers watched in silence until the main branch broke off and sailed towards them, hovering atop Kilfer. The villagers gasped and murmured softly amongst each other, but only Otnoybsk paid no heed to the threat, "Catch them!" The man holding the chains paused for a moment, glancing uneasily at the branch hovering atop them, and Kilfer took the opportunity to escape.

"Come!" Kilfer leaped into the air and grabbed Mirdaff's hand, using a gust of wind to propel them away from the village. It didn't matter to them how the villagers saw them, but they were now free, and Kilfer had a mission to accomplish.

Chapter 17

Kilfer landed with Mirdaff, and they surveyed the landscape. They were on a cliff that was splattered with snow on its plain grey stone, and through the velvety cold mist they saw dragons, huge as they were and fire-breathing, amber eyes filled with the pride and grace of being a flying worm, but what they feared were the mountains, living rocks that were powerful beings that were the souls of mountains and can kill whenever they wanted, and judging by the number of dragons they were also not far from the Fire Dragons' Lair, home to the fiercest beings ever known in their history.

"Kilfer," Mirdaff glanced up from the map, "It is dangerous, only through these living mountain bastards can we continue our paths. It does not help if we get to the air, for the dragons would consume us alive."

Kilfer sighed but he knew what should be done must be done. They continued across the ledge from the cliff, crossing a winding pathway that was once built by someone but wore off so much it was barely visible, and linking the ledge to the first living mountain was a bridge, torn to the sides and without rungs, but moving from side to side whenever the wind blew.

Kilfer gulped. Never in his life did he need to do something so risky and he would have glided to the other end of the mountain if not for the dragons. Clutching the box that held Ferhia within, he took a single step. The bridge wobbled and he inhaled deeply."Ferhia, aid me, please. I will proceed with my instinct, but to my luck only you can help me," Kilfer shut his eyes tight and raised his hands, balancing Ferhia's box on one hand and the other was a free hand. Within Kilfer's senses, there was entirely no sound, and he took continuous steps across the bridge, every step filled with uncertainty for there was a tingling sensation of fear that at any moment if simply a small wind tipped the bridge by that tiny amount it might mean his death.

Finally, he stepped onto an unwavering piece of ground and opened his eyes. Finally, he was on the other side of the bridge and opened his eyes. He turned and flew Mirdaff with his magic to his side across the bridge.

None of them spoke, for they knew any sound would cause the mountains to know of their presence, and through the mists they could see rocks moving, mountains hurling rocks at each other and smashing huge boulders, and they knew they could not continue any further without flying.

"We fly...?" Kilfer mouthed with uncertainty, but Mirdaff shook his head, "No, it would be death too."

They continued in silence and walked along ledges and leapt across cliffs, until Kilfer accidentally made a grave mistake -- tripping over a pebble that made too much noise and the living mountain under their feet trembled and moved through the air while they clung onto whatever that they could hold on to, and the trembles stopped. Kilfer and Mirdaff froze, staring at each other for a moment. They thought that it was over, but before any of them could take another breath, a crack widened from the ground, revealing a gaping hole and it swallowed them whole.

***

"Where are..." Kilfer wanted to speak, but paused when he saw that he was in a stone room, walls crumbling to the sides but Kilfer knew that they were trapped by the living mountain, waiting to kill them by starving them within in this labyrinth. Few had ever escaped, and those who actually escaped did not live long enough to tell the full story and how to escape the stony prison. Yet now, escaping was their only chance.Kilfer and Mirdaff stood, surveying the smooth stone surface, and it was so clean Kilfer thought it was artificial, but they knew it was simply another part of the labyrinth within the mountains. "So what now?" Mirdaff turned to Kilfer and Kilfer realised he was also pondering on that question, and simply shrugged, "I guess there should be an opening somewhere. The problem simply is that the labyrinth is alive, and all we can do is try to prevent ourselves from dying in here while we seek a way out.

"Mirdaff slipped his hand lightly across the wall, trying to find a hole or any sort, but Kilfer had just found a method of his own. He already felt magic within the mountain that kept the mountain alive. Yet powerful with the magic, the mountains could be rivalled easily with his own magic. Pressing hard on the cold wall Kilfer injected a pulse if magic, and let it seep into every inch of the wall and felt the magic. As the magic passed through all the walls and other rooms and secret passages of the labyrinth he could picture the entire labyrinth with his mind, and Kilfer ejected a deadly force within the rock, and while the living mountains' magic could not stop it the stone wall broke into chunks in front of him, finally revealing a tunnel that stretched into the darkness. "Follow me!" Kilfer beckoned to Mirdaff and they sprinted out of the room, while behind them another crackling of stone could be heard, and the next time they turned around the wall that had been blasted apart by Kilfer was back to its original position, as if no one touched it before.

"You're right, Kilfer... this labyrinth is trying to trap us," Mirdaff spoke, and Kilfer could feel Mirdaff shaking even from his voice. They were within the tunnel now, it was all velvety black and there was only a single option: going forward. Every ounce of their breath echoed against the walls and around them was an annoying silence as they tiptoed within the darkness, trying to make their way through mutely, for Kilfer's previous mistake had told them to keep as silent as possible.

The tunnel turned to a smaller chamber that extended out into the darkness, and Kilfer paused, feeling a knot of anxiety in his stomach, and he felt that something was about to happen, lurking in the darkness, just about to leap out of its hiding hole and have their souls ripped from their mortal selves...

Kilfer decided it was not really a wise choice to continue, for his sixth sense was accurate with his magic, and he reached forward to Mirdaff to stop him but it was a little too late, for a low growling sound of rusted metal made his blood freeze to ice, and from the darkness a huge iron boulder slammed across the walls towards them and Kilfer pulled Mirdaff out of harms' way, but he could not feel Mirdaff's hands anymore, and when the boulder passed them, Kilfer found out that he was alone and Mirdaff disappeared totally without a trace.

Kilfer stood slowly, and spoke, "Mirdaff?" His voice echoed into the darkness, and after a few moments a voice, unmistakeably Mirdaff's, "Kilfer! Where are you?"

"Where are you, that's my question!" Kilfer yelled and noticed the reply seemed to emanate from a distant location, "Somewhere... I don't know but it seems I'm trapped. I'm floating, I'm weightless, I can't move."

"I'm coming, just continue to speak to me and I will get to you," Kilfer yelled into the darkness, trying to detect where Mirdaff's voice is coming from. He continued into the tunnel, catching every syllable from Mirdaff and deciding between two separate routes when it branched out, and soon he was already so accustomed to the darkness he simply sniffed the air and heard Mirdaff's voice to continue, and made no hesitation even when he was robbed of his sight.

***

Mirdaff's grip slipped on Kilfer's the moment he heard the iron boulder rolling down towards them. The ground opened and everything happened so quickly, but the last thing his conscious self remembered was him sliding down a smooth slide, and the next thing he knew, he tumbled out of the darkness onto a stone, and when he stood warm air billowed onto his face. Mirdaff realized that he was simply standing on a chunk of stone that was one of many in a hall, and beneath the stone lava bubbled, the heat searing him and seemed to be tearing his skin apart even though his skin was not even near the lava. His vision blurred, but he could still see a grotto barely a few metres away from him.

'It's now or never,' Mirdaff thought to himself for he knew that the mountains could make the stone beneath him give way and that would be the end of him -- unless he leapt toward the grotto that he thought was the only possibility of safety for him. Taking a deep breath, he gathered all the strength and leapt. For a moment his body was in the air, and then he landed, his wooden shoes slamming the ground just in front of the grotto with such force he lost his balance and tumbled over into the gaping entrance. Then, his body felt weightless, and he was suspended horizontally within the air. He could not feel the ground beneath him, and it seemed as if he was surrounded by nothingness, empty space, yet the darkness within the empty space seemed to be menacing, consuming him whole, paralyzing him. He became unable to move, unable to feel the ground, trapped within the darkness."Mirdaff?" He heard Kilfer's voice reverberate across the walls if there were even any walls in that open space that was so dark he wasn't even sure if it was a grotto itself.

"Kilfer! Where are you?" Mirdaff yelled into the darkness.

The conversation continued, but with every syllable, Mirdaff spoke he felt even more lethargic until he needed to strain even to breathe. The air around him seemed to gain the weight of lead, pushing down against him and seemed to be cracking every bone within his body as he floated across the weightless space...

Chapter 18

"Mirdaff?" Kilfer tried to seek a reply, but there was still silence.

He sighed. He was already so close, and when he was just so near to Mirdaff, he stopped speaking and Kilfer could only rely on his senses to guide him and where he felt Mirdaff's pulsating lifeforce was. Yet with every throb, his lifeforce seemed to be getting weaker and weaker, and it felt as if it would stop altogether even when the slightest of winds blew.

Then a roar stopped him in his tracks and he stood rooted to the ground. It was so loud it rocked the tunnel he was walking in and seemed to be coming from the darkness in front of him. A dragon. A cave dragon. Kilfer thought, then immediately corrected himself, for those that lurked in caves and fed on mice were much deadlier than any of the rest. Another roar echoed in the distance, and Kilfer feared for Mirdaff's safety and felt his lifeforce. It was concealed within another cave, yet something told him that it was far more dangerous in the cave than it was to be with the dragon.

Slipping towards where the tunnel widened to a grotto Kilfer tensed, and he glanced from behind a stone wall. There it lay, the fearsome beast covered in plates of gold and fiery amber lava erupting from under his throat with its every breath, ravenous and deadly.

Kilfer surveyed the monster from its tail up, and to its body until his eyes glanced at its vermillion eyes for that very brief moment, and it turned towards him, glaring at him. Right after the moment their eyes met, Kilfer whipped his head behind the wall, but a moment too late. Kilfer knew it already saw him, and from the way the ground shook Kilfer could sense that the monster was gaining on him.

"Save me please, Ferhia. I trust you, my sister," Kilfer squeezed the box and placed it in the ground lightly, and stepped out from behind the wall, and finally, he could see the dragon as they faced each other.

Kilfer reached out to the surroundings and pulled on the rocks, and it easily gave way, a huge chunk of rock breaking away and sailing towards the dragon, but it simply broke into tiny pieces and rained down harmlessly down the scales the moment it impacted them, while the dragon glowered, its jaws widened and from behind his throat crimson light flared, and flames licked the air out of his throat towards him. He leaped aside, behind a boulder, but already felt the heat sting his hands, and when he glanced down his forearms they were burnt, charred and numb.

"You shall never escape me," The dragon spoke, its raspy voice like a thousand claws scraping a wall, "You are merely delaying the inevitable."

When Kilfer peeped over the boulder, the dragon was just in front of the boulder, slowly advancing, right about to pounce, every indestructible scale heaving with power and madness, it seemed as though it was totally unable to be slain -- until he saw the throat of the dragon. It's only weakness. The dragon used its throat to eject fire, its most powerful weapon, yet it was the most vulnerable spot. The only soft spot that could be harmed.

"Aid me," Kilfer whispered and hoped Ferhia's spirit would help him, and broke a long, thin piece of stone and aimed, while the dragon inched closer.

Thirty feet.

Twenty feet.

Ten feet.

Kilfer hurled the stone shaft as hard as he could, and it plunged itself deep into its throat. The dragon paused in its tracks and tensed. For a moment both human and dragon stopped moving, and the gargantuan creature crashed to the ground, its eyes unmoving and staring at Kilfer, but its slow breaths told Kilfer that it is still alive, but only injured.

Grabbing Ferhia's box, Kilfer scrambled towards the opening which he felt Mirdaff was and felt for Mirdaff's lifeforce within. It was still there, but so weak and fragile that showed how near

Mirdaff was to dying; it was simply dull throbs that he could not feel without pausing to focus. Yet he felt something more within the opening, much powerful and concentrated magic from within that was crushing Mirdaff, both his lifeforce and his mortal self.

Kilfer gathered all his magic and forced it into the entrance, letting it rush into the dark void beyond. He was still surprised how his magic had grown since the day he left the Lair for the Swamps, and now he could even let his magic take a form of itself, as golden wisps of velvety strands that were powerful enough to resist the magic within the void in front of him now.

The magic reached out to Mirdaff and tugged him slowly out of the darkness within. Finally, Mirdaff appeared, his face pale and white and his eyes closed, and Kilfer bent down and placed a palm on his icy cold forehead, and the magic entered him, the magic of warmth and life that he knew would exhaust him out but he still continued, watching silently as the thin wisps of golden magic entered Mirdaff and disappeared beneath his skin, and soon he could feel the warmth returning, his hands started to move and his eyes fluttered open.

"Where are we?" Mirdaff sat up and glanced at Kilfer.

Kilfer paused to think of what reply he should provide, and in the end, Kilfer decided not to answer his question directly, "We are safe. There's still a journey ahead of us, we'd better be quick."Mirdaff nodded and stood, and the duo left the grotto, while Kilfer turned back for a brief moment to study the opening to the void and shuddered. It was unnerving that even such weak magic could prove fatal to a human-like Mirdaff, and he could not imagine how much harm the darkness and The Ghost from beyond the veil could do to all the mortal creatures living in this world.

"Here!" Mirdaff jabbed at a wall, and Kilfer noticed light emanating out of it. Finally, they would be about to escape this labyrinth of destruction, and he broke a larger part of the wall for them to climb through. Finally, they were free, even though suspended on a ledge Kilfer felt comfort to be out of the darkness. Yet the terrain beyond seemed alien. The snow-capped landscape was totally different from the greenish forests and canyons that they saw before they entered the labyrinth, but they could still make out where they were and inched forward slowly. The dim light from the sun, covered mostly by the mist and snow was still overhead and they still had a couple of hours to get to a resting place before night arrived. The mountains they stood on were still alive for quite a long time until they sailed the wind across the canyon to another mountain where a blizzard was still howling in vicious demeanor.

"Mirdaff," Kilfer staggered behind a rock and the other followed suit, and Kilfer took out the map with shaky hands, "Where are we now?"Mirdaff studied the map and pinpointed a place, quite near to their destination, "Here, this is called the frozen wastelands. Nothing lies here except for blizzards and the never-ending cold, that means we should be safe from any bloodthirsty creatures or whatsoever."

Kilfer thought about it. To get back to the warmer side of the mountains they would need to journey across three mountains again, and there was a possibility that they could get eaten by dragons, but even the colder path seemed shorter and less deadly from the map, one question still remained: Would they be able to survive the cold?

Kilfer noticed both Mirdaff and himself had the color of their cheeks were drained, and if they continued they might not survive the cold. His magic allowed him to control physical objects, but to the extent of summoning fire or ice or doing anything of that level, Kilfer could not."I don't think that would be a possible way," Kilfer shook his head, "The cold is dangerous, and the ice is more likely to freeze you than warmth is to harm you, Mirdaff. We cannot continue with this route. "But it's longer that way!" Mirdaff protested, but the moment he spoke another icy cold gust blew across their faces. The duo shuddered and Mirdaff fell silent.

After a long moment of staring blindly into the white land-scape, the last rays of the sun dipped below the horizon. It was nighttime, and it was already useless to continue their journey so they laid down to rest, but in such a harsh temperature they woke up countless time in the middle of the night to find out that the snow had covered them to their waists and they had to brush it off. Yet, in a ragged dream, Kilfer seemed to hear

Mizervon calling out to him above the wind of the blizzard, "Come, child. Come to me, come..."

Chapter 19

By dawn, the blizzard had subsided and the duo staggered forward through the white desolate wasteland, with Mirdaff still adhering to his idea of cutting through the snowy mountains. Their lips were cracked and mouths were parched, bits of snow clinging to their tunic and face, the cold biting deep into their skin.

With every step they took they left a mark on the white plains, the footprints etched deep into the snow. The route was slow and painful, they could only see barely a few feet from where they were and the frost-biting weather did not help them at all.

Finally, they stopped in their tracks as the mist cleared and they finally could see into the distance, an entire canyon filled with snow that seemed to have rested there for ages, silent and untouched, and they had finally reached a cliff and beyond it lies the entire canyon, outstretched across the scenery they could see. But beyond the spirit-like serenity lies something else, a thick mist that shielded what was beyond from their eyes, and the dark wall of mystery extended up into the skies, blocking all light beyond. "That is... unnerving," Mirdaff whispered, his eyes still fixated on the wall of darkness.

"That sure is," Kilfer replied. They did not expect what lay at the end for them was this, yet what was beyond the wall of mist, they had to find out.

"So... we continue?" Mirdaff glanced uneasily into the distance.

Kilfer nodded but signaled for Mirdaff to wait and crouched under the sand. Mirdaff wanted to speak but Kilfer placed a finger on his lips, glancing into the snow. Then, the entire serene white blanket of snow erupted in front of them, drifting higher and higher until a path was formed connecting both sides of the canyon, the width of the canyon a few feet apart from each other and snow itself was moulded together so flawlessly that the surface was smooth from where they could see. Under the bridge, from the cold, unpigmented snow something welled up from within, so crystalline and pure, little pools of water finally forming. From beneath the snow around them, bits of green started popping out, and soon the entire canyon was filled with life. Even Kilfer could not understand how he managed to create such a magnificent canyon from sea of snowy loneliness when he simply wanted to create a bridge for them to pass, but that was magic. It delves beneath the monotonous unappealing view to the eye and pulls out the beauty buried deep underneath.

"Wow," Mirdaff awed, "You did all of this?"Kilfer shook his head. "It wasn't me. I only control magic, but to who -- or what -- did all this, it is magic. It is not anything to marvel about for it is the soul of nature, a veil around all things that causes change in everything, including birth, growth and even death. It is here, within and beyond us."

Kilfer remembered what the Alpha told him, yet as he told Mirdaff all he learned throughout the years of practicing magic, he was still filled with doubt to these words he had just uttered. It just did not make sense how magic could lie within every soul, and be the constructing bricks for life itself.

Seeing Mirdaff's bewildered face, Kilfer shook his head, "Never mind, we've got to continue."

They continued across the bridge and ventured towards the wall filled with dark mist, their footprints sinking deep into the snow and their feet were freezing from the cold and felt numb and lifeless. With every step, the dark wall loomed closer and closer, and finally covered them overhead and into the distance, they could already see the snow narrowing, giving way to sand and a few shrubs.

Kilfer felt the air getting warmer, and he could smell... the sea. It was a peculiar smell of salt and he had not smelt it for a long time. The continued until they were right in front of the wall of mists, the thick gas swirling in front of them. Kilfer signaled for Kilfer to wait, and reached out to brush across the mist in a fluid manner. How dark it appeared, the mist felt the same as air, just darker, and when he reached onto the ground within the mist, a surge of water rushed between his fingers, cold and refreshing.

"It's water," Kilfer turned to Mirdaff, "I think it should be a lake... a sea, possibly. Follow me, hold my hand, let's go."

The duo ventured into the water, Kilfer staggering in front and Mirdaff trailing behind, holding each other's hands and Kilfer grabbing his hand and the box that contained Ferhia together. At first, the cold liquid was at shin level but afterwards deepened until it reached their ankles and waists, until Kilfer felt that Mirdaff's hands were shaking.

"Cold?" Kilfer asked, and Mirdaff simply answered with a chatter, "Y...yes."

Kilfer contemplated what he could do. They were too far into the water to go back up on land, but when trapped within this inky darkness and icy water he knew he and Mirdaff would freeze to death if they were not quick, and how he felt that he could not use his magic within the mist is unnerving when he just could not use his magic to his own will.

He continued into the water until his body hit something hard, solid and drifting on the water. He tensed and reached forward. When he felt the object with the hand not clinging to Mirdaff and the box that contained Ferhia, and found that it was a long, smooth piece of wood that resembled the shape of a boat through touch.

"Mirdaff," Kilfer whispered into the darkness and squeezed his hand, "I think I've found something."

"W...what?" Came Mirdaff's shaky voice.

"A boat, I believe," Kilfer tried to climb over the piece of wood, and after quite a few tries he tumbled onto the wooden boat that rocked quite severely, and hauled Mirdaff out of the freezing water.

"What the... why is there a boat here?" Mirdaff said as they tried to get their tunic dry, "I mean, why would there be a boat here outta nowhere?"

"I don't know," Kilfer replied, shrugging, "But just consider ourselves lucky, not everyone gets a boat like that."

They used their hands as oars, propelling the boat through the still water, and they lost track of direction and time in the darkness, and they could only rely on their gut feeling to lead them on. Kilfer's hands ached, and the numbness soared everytime his hands swept across the water it felt like pinpricks on his palm.

Finally, they were too tired to continue that Mirdaff stopped propelling the boat with his hands and let the boat lead itself across the water, and Kilfer stopped soon after, and what followed was silence. Kilfer was about to doze off when a blinding light hit him and he opened his eyes to find the sun glaring down at them, the wall of mist receding from behind them, and their faces and tunic were blackened and they were still drifting calmly on the boat.

"Kilfer," He heard Mirdaff's voice call him and sat up. "Where are we? Are we... safe?"

Kilfer glanced around, and they seemed to be in the middle of nowhere on a vast ocean, but they were still not safe. Kilfer could feel his magic rising within him back again, but his stomach hurt so badly that they had nothing to eat and barely anything to drink (except for the seawater that allowed them survival) for the past one and a half days that he could barely summon water to his will. He could see Mirdaff's sunken cheeks and lifeless expression, and they were desperately in need of food, or they would die.

They were still unsafe.

"Maybe," Kilfer replied, "If hope still lies in front of us. If there is land beyond us, and we are drifting towards it, probably we are safe." Kilfer glanced towards the horizon. It was filled with water until the very ends, which seemed utterly merciless to him.

"Kilfer," A voice made him jump. The voice was not alien to him, yet he still could not believe that he would yet again hear the voice, and he glanced up at where the voice came from in surprise.

"Bronswig!" Kilfer cried as he glanced into the dwarf's eyes. The dwarfish figure glanced down at him, but he found out something weird, translucent with a bluish hue around him.

Kilfer glanced behind to Mirdaff, and Mirdaff seemed to pay no heed to the dwarf's presence.

"You aren't here," Kilfer spoke with a sense of realization and stood. He really hoped that the dwarf was with him, to aid him when he was about to perish in this maelstrom of calm and silence, yet there seemed to be no hope now. He was simply a figure that was only a memory of his, so surreal and close, yet so far.

"You seem to be giving up, huh?" The dwarf spoke, ignoring Kilfer. Kilfer decided to stay silent towards Bronswig. After a long moment of silence, Bronswig continued, "You never know what is beyond this horizon, possibly what is waiting at the end in the hope that you desperately seek now, but to whether you can achieve it or not... it is up to you."

Bronswig reached out, but when his hands touched Kilfer's, it simply passed through him. However, he felt energy rush through him at that moment, and he could not feel his hunger and thirst but felt his magic welling up within him, and he could feel the water beneath him and sense the direction and navigate through the waters. He shut his eyes tight and for that brief moment he saw land, and within the land, he felt magic so strong and so vibrant that it outshone the sun, and the richness in the ground rejuvenated all the creatures that resided on that island.

Kilfer opened his eyes, but Bronswig -- or his spirit -- was gone. But now he was filled with determination, he knew that something was waiting for him at the end, and he could not afford to stop and give up. Not now at least.

Kilfer stood, and thrust his arms forward, and a surge of water hit the boat roughly, propelling it forward and spraying freezing water all around them.

"Come, Mirdaff! Let's ride the waves!" Kilfer yelled over the roar of the waves, summoning an even larger wave that nearly capsized the boat, and when the speed of the boat stabilized, Kilfer finally sat back on the boat heavily.

"Mirdaff," Kilfer finally turned towards Mirdaff, breathing heavily, "We have hope. I saw land in front of us. We have hope!"

Mirdaff smiled forcefully, but Kilfer could see the hunger and thirst within his eyes. Kilfer knew that Mirdaff had not eaten for a long time, and his cheeks were robbed of color and he was so thin he seemed as if he was a mere skeleton, only with skin wrapped around it.

"Here, Mirdaff," Kilfer reached out and took Mirdaff's hand, and water flowed from Kilfer to Mirdaff in an unexplainable way, and when Kilfer finally stopped he found the color on Mirdaff's face returning.

"Feeling better?" Kilfer asked.

"Yes, but how..."

"The work of nature," Kilfer grinned, then turned back to his navigation, "I believe we should let this boat speed up, there is still a long way for the land lies at the edge of this ocean.

Drifting like this will never help, but the only way to let this speed up is to let the waves guide it along."

Kilfer stood and tried his best to move to the other side of the boat without capsizing it, and placed a hand into the water, and he focused for a moment, digging into the darkest, inkiest depths of the sea and forcing an entire current up to them, every single bit of water replied to his summon, and he had barely time to turn back and shout to Mirdaff, "Be careful!" when the sea seemed to explode around them, the entire sea of water driving them forward violently, and Kilfer could only grasp onto the boat with one hand and Ferhia's box with another hand.

The waves surged on, and the wind roared on his face, he did not know how Mirdaff was handling it but by sensing his lifeforce, Kilfer knew Mirdaff was still on the boat with him.

The tumultuous waves ensued, battling the tiny boat as Kilfer used his magic to will it on, driving them forward. Yet, he felt the island getting further, away from his grasp and again a wave of uneasiness washed over him.

"Please, Mizervon," Kilfer spoke into the wind, "If you are still here -- and I believe you are -- let me meet you. This is simply for the good, for all the living beings, spirits, and even magic itself, please... let me see you for once..."

Then the wind stopped, the sounds of the waves eroded into silence and he could not feel the water anymore. He was numb, but he knew he was on the boat with Mirdaff.

Kilfer opened his eyes, and the boat was already on an island filled with a leafy paradise, the forest filled with a powerful strength that seemed to have the strength of a thousand suns, yet the strongest magic lay in a cliff reaching out to the skies, a huge figure of a knight carved onto it, and from the downward pointing sword a waterfall replaced its blade, the water resembling the shimmering blade of the sword, reflecting the soft glow of daylight.

"What... just happened?" Kilfer heard Mirdaff speak, and turned to Mirdaff and saw him struggling to climb out of the boat.

"I communicated with Mizervon, and he brought us right... here," Kilfer replied, grabbing Ferhia's box and clambered out of the boat.

"So what do we do now?" Mirdaff asked, glancing up at the cliff, "Do we climb that thing or what?"

Kilfer shrugged and continued strolling towards the sea of green, "I don't think climbing is really that fast. How about flying there?"

Mirdaff glanced at him warily, but Kilfer simply grinned, "Come, it'll be fun!"

***

Kilfer extended his hands and summoned a huge gust of wind. On one hand, he held Ferhia's box which was considerably heavy on one hand, and on his back, Mirdaff clung tight.

"Here we go!" Kilfer yelled and launched himself into the air, and laughed in excitement. He had always loved the sensation when he was flying, where there was totally no constraints to what he could do. The breeze turned to gusts of wind that rippled across them, and the view of the entire island spread in front of them.

Kilfer did a somersault in the air and was preparing for a nosedive onto the mountain but felt Mirdaff cling even tighter to him and remembered that he had a passenger, and slowed down.

"You okay? Sorry I might have scared you there," Kilfer spoke as he glided down, but there was no reply from Mirdaff so he thought Mirdaff might be too fearful to speak. Finally, the huge carving of the knight on the cliff face was right in front of them, and Kilfer tried to search for a crevice to land on.

"I see an opening there!" Mirdaff jabbed suddenly to the sword that was carved onto the cliff face with the knight, and Kilfer saw it -- right under the hilt of the carving where the waterfall started cascading down to a lake below the cliff. The opening was not huge, with only a tiny ledge outside the opening, and Kilfer tried to land thrice but only to have his feet skid right off the ledge, and only barely managed to land on the fourth try.

Within the mountain, there was no light but Kilfer could summon a small flame on his hand as a glimmer of light. It was a tunnel that wound down the mountain in circles and made the entire descent seem annoyingly long, but finally, they could smell the peculiarly fragrant scent of flowers across the tunnel, yet the only thing they could see for a long time was still darkness.

Chapter 20

K ilfer was deep in thought.

He had come so far from the Edge to this island which he never knew existed, just to earn hope for himself, for Ferhia, and for Mirdaff. He was so close, yet if everything was not real, if the tunnel they were walking to was a dead end? What if Bronswig lied to him all along, and the darkness was destined to usurp all he loved... what if Ferhia's prophecy was true all along?

Kilfer did not dare think further. Perhaps Mirdaff knew about the darkness, but he would never have known how dangerous they were, and the future of all the realms rested on their hands.

Then, Kilfer paused. He heard something as soft as the tiniest breeze that whistled across his ears, music that was so soft it was barely audible.

Behind, Mirdaff bumped onto him.

"Why did you stop?" Mirdaff asked but Kilfer turned back and placed a finger on his lips. Mirdaff immediately fell silent, but when Kilfer went back to listen, the music was no more.

Kilfer walked on in agitation that he had lost the music, but as he rounded a bend he saw a ray of orange light bouncing off the walls that illuminated what was in front. He slowed down and glanced ahead, and the tunnel widened out to an entire hall at the first glance but was more like a shaft when Kilfer finally stepped out.

There was no ground, and what Kilfer stepped on was only a ledge, and it opened up to an empty void beneath. When he glanced up, the blue skies were the only thing above him. The shaft seemed to lead to nowhere when he saw an opening on the stone face on the opposite side.

"Mirdaff," Kilfer spoke as Mirdaff came out of the tunnel behind him, "We are here, and the only way forward is the entrance there." Kilfer jabbed at the opening on the opposite side and Mirdaff saw it immediately.

"No! I'm not going flying with you again," Mirdaff shook his head, "Especially when it is a void below!"

"I don't mean that," Kilfer said, "No one said we're going flying. Look carefully."

Mirdaff stared at the entrance and Kilfer himself was also quite amazed to find the way to the entrance across the shaft, it was a thin stick connecting between the two ends of the shaft, the same colour, and shade as the stone wall of the shaft that

Kilfer could barely make out the stick that was barely as thick as one of his foot.

"What? I see the opening, but there's nothing else," Mirdaff turned to Kilfer, frowning skeptically.

"I'll show you. Watch," Kilfer walked to the stick and placed a foot on the stick. He did not know why he chose not to simply fly to the other side, but he knew he could only walk for flying to the other side in such an enclosed space with a void below is dangerous, perhaps a fatal choice. Yet, while walking on the stick his life was also at stake, for any wrong step would result in him plummeting down into the darkness below.

Kilfer took another step. His foot landed on the stick. He held out his hands for balance, and the darkness below seemed to be extending its grasp towards him, slowly tugging him down. Kilfer did not know if it was simply a figment of his imagination or something else, but looked up and continued. On his outstretched hands, the weight of Ferhia in the box strained his strength and there was no support. It was just his determination and the void.

With every step, the entrance grew closer, and he could hear music and see light emanating from within. He felt comfort from the warmth of the orange light and hope from the simple melody.

"Kilfer!" He heard Mirdaff shout, "I'm coming!"

Kilfer did not reply. He did not want Mirdaff to walk behind him for he feared that Mirdaff might fall any moment, yet he could not utter a word for his life was at stake too.

Kilfer felt Mirdaff's weight on the stick. It shook a little with every step they took. It was so unstable, and it felt as if the thin, long piece of stone would snap under their combined weight at any moment...

The entrance was right in front of Kilfer now, he counted barely ten steps to the opening, and the dim light could already be seen, and the music was finally audible, louder than he expected. That was the first time he heard such music, sounds produced out of thin air, more magic than mimed voices.

The thin stone beneath him shook again. He felt it was getting unstable and it might break beneath their combined weight anytime unless he reached the other side in time...

Kilfer leaped forward. It was very risky, but he landed successfully at the mouth of the opening. He turned and found Mirdaff struggling on the thin stone.

"Need some help?" Kilfer yelled, and Mirdaff nodded. Kilfer focused on Mirdaff and lifted him into the air with magic and brought him through the air and placed him down beside him. Mirdaff's face was white, his knuckles the same color and he was shaking.

"C'mon, don't try walking on that yourself," Kilfer spoke, "Anyway, I believe we have reached our destination."

Kilfer's voice was filled with confidence, but below his strength, he was filled with uncertainty. No one knew better than Mizervon himself if they had really reached their destination, and he feared if it was a dead end, then all their hopes have come to naught.

The duo continued into the tunnel and it widened to an opening that led them out into the open. Nothing could have prepared them to what they were about to see, for the moment they stepped out an eagle with golden feathers streaked across their heads, landing on a tree on their right. In front, a slope lay dressed with flowers, and trees with leaves that glowed a bluish hue. A thin passageway cut across the slope to the top, revealing something like a door that they could not clearly make out there.

"Wow," Mirdaff was still staring at the trees and flowers, transfixed by its beauty, "This must be where Mizervon resided all these years, and this must be the work of art of Mizervon's magic! No other magician could paint nature in such an exquisite way!"

"Magic," Kilfer repeated slowly and deliberate manner. Mizervon's powers and grasp of magic meant that there is still hope for the light. The most powerful glimmer of light resides on this very slope that Kilfer stood on, thoughts raced through his mind as both boys sauntered up the slope, finally reaching a huge door made of jade, and Kilfer reached out towards the doorknob to open the door, yet it opened right before his hands touched the doorknob.

They stepped in slowly, and there was a cool breeze blew from inside just as they stepped in, and inside they found that it was a hall, much more spacious than it seemed outside, and at the sides of the hall there were seven granite statues of different men in different positions, some wielding a sword in battle and some in a robe, holding a cup of wine. On the opposite side of the hall, a huge altar of the Wolf God dwarfed any other object in the hall, and in front of the altar, a lone figure in an umber cloak sat, unmoving.

"Mizervon," Kilfer spoke, slowly walking towards the figure. He turned, and the moment he faced Kilfer, Kilfer saw the deep yellow eyes of a magician, his magic honed to perfection through thousands of years of deep practice, with a beard that cascaded down to the floor below him, and beneath his cloak was only a simple robe the color of ash.

"You have finally come, great human leader of the Pack," Mizervon spoke, his voice strangled as he stood, "And you have brought a friend. A young but worthy friend, hmm? Welcome to the Hall of the Seven Kings, the center of magic and power that holds the tombs of the Seven Kings that helped the Pack and defended the realm with them a thousand years ago."

"Yes, I am Kilfer and my friend here is Mirdaff, but I come to you not to chat over tea. Something has happened," Kilfer decided to leap to the issue, but Mizervon simply swatted Kilfer off, "Nah, I already know about it. Ferhia's curse, the death of the Pack and the darkness being released from behind the veil. I see all and hear all, what makes you think that I do not know of such an important happening?"

"What? You knew..." Kilfer was suddenly filled with annoyance. Why did he not save Ferhia then, and why did he not save the Pack then? Why did he let Bronswig sacrifice himself against the darkness?

Mizervon seemed to sense Kilfer's annoyance towards him and spoke, "When I vowed to Wolf God, I swore I would not step out of this island or I will get killed by the darkness, and that exchanged my immortality. I did not have a choice, you see. Oh, I also created all beyond the wall of mist and added the boat for your safety. In fact, I did not want you to come, I wanted you to lose confidence but in the end, I knew that I had to give in."

Kilfer decided to keep quiet, and after a long, awkward moment Mizervon finally spoke, "Come, give me the box and we'll see what we can do to help your sister."

Kilfer released his grasp on the box the held Ferhia and it sailed through the air towards Mizervon, who then caught it mid-air and placed it in front of him. Mizervon opened it and there Ferhia was, and Mizervon took her out of the box, where Ferhia enlarged to her full size.

Kilfer and Mirdaff rushed forward towards Mizervon, and finally saw Ferhia's face, cold and white, lying as still as stone.

Dead. Mizervon, however, did not seem too affected that a corpse lay in front of him and placed a hand on top of Ferhia's face, speaking chants in the Wolf tongue.

Mirdaff and Kilfer watched in tense silence as Mizervon reached into his tunic pocket and took out a red powder and sprinkled it lightly on Ferhia's tunic, and looked up slowly. Even before Mizervon spoke Kilfer knew that he could not save Ferhia, and Mizervon spoke, sighing, "Her lifeforce is within her body, she isn't fully dead yet, but I can't revive her unless the darkness stays within the Swamps, for Ferhia's spirit is covered with dark magic and she could not return to her mortal body."

"Then... if we succeed in exterminating the darkness, we can revive my sister?"

Mizervon nodded.

"Please," Kilfer spoke, "Save her, please. I can't let her just lie like this in front of my eyes. I can't let the darkness usurp all that I loved!"

"You see," Mizervon said, "I am weak and frail, no matter how powerful my magic is my mortal body is so weak I might not stand even a blow from the darkness, let alone fight against waves and waves of the madness. Now it is your time. You can lead all the world's beings and spirits into the battle that will determine the fate of the lands. There are magicians in the cities of the humans, and most have already prepared for battle, but I can see that with those mere skills their magic is totally useless against the darkness. They are hoping for me to arrive and exterminate them, and if you arrive they will listen and aid you against the fury of the darkness. About where you will achieve such powerful magic... I will pass the magic on to you."

Mizervon stood, "Come on, young lad. We've got tasks on hand."

Kilfer and Mirdaff followed him up a flight of stairs from a corner of the hall. Yet Kilfer was filled with nervousness, for he did not know who -- or what would become of him after he received Mizervon's magic.

Chapter 21

Kilfer and Mirdaff followed Mizervon up to an iron door and it swung open without Mizervon even touching it. They went in, and it was a simple room with gray walls and a circular mat placed on the ground in the middle of the room.

"Come, Kilfer. Sit," Mizervon instructed, pointing at the mat and Kilfer did as told.

"Close your eyes," Mizervon spoke again and Kilfer did so.

In the darkness, he waited for the next instruction to come, but instead, there was a painful feeling surging up his spine, right up to his brain and it ached so much his entire body was numb with pain. Kilfer winced and hoped for Mizervon to tell him that it is alright, but there was no comforting voice. Just the darkness and the pain.

Then, something washed over him, something... peculiar yet filled with power, so strong that his body felt so heavy when the magic rushed through him.

Then, everything stopped. In front of Kilfer was a blank whiteness, and the pain was gone, so was the powerful swelling sensation. Yet he sensed something different, that his body had changed on a larger scale, a scale that he could not imagine. He felt stronger, although not yet infinite, he felt powerful magic rushing through his veins.

Kilfer opened his eyes. In front of him, Mizervon sat, looking at him silently. Mirdaff stood beside him and seemed to be a little shaken.

"What... happened?" Kilfer could barely stutter.

"Your face was turning purple, and your hair became so white as if you... you died at that very instant the magic entered you," Mirdaff spoke.

"So," Mizervon ignored Mirdaff, "You like the feel of your newly acquired powers? Whether you like it or not, the darkness has broken the barriers Bronswig created from his life-force. It has already spread through ten cities, with more than a hundred thousand lives lost already. Kilfer, the fate of all depends on you. Go now."

Mizervon snapped his fingers twice, and the surroundings changed. The cold gray walls that surrounded them unfurled like a piece of paper to reveal the skies overhead. The sun was nearly dipping down the horizon, and they were standing on a platform high above the slope that they could see the entire island itself.

"Go now, Kilfer," Mizervon said, "Fly towards the darkness as fast as you can. Fight them."

Kilfer soared into the sky. It felt effortless, and as he continued further and further into the clouds Mizervon turned back to Mirdaff, "Come, young lad. Let's talk."

***

Mizervon and Mirdaff were back at the Hall of the Seven Kings, and they spoke while Mizervon prepared some dreamwine for both of them.

"You know," Mizervon shrugged, grinning, "White lies have to be told. I did not tell Kilfer about my real abilities. I could fight the darkness, but I simply wanted him to take my place here in the Hall of the Seven Kings, and you shall aid him. He must learn to use his acquired magic, and he must learn to fight the darkness."

"What?" Came Mirdaff's startled reply, "So you could fight? But you said..."

Mizervon chuckled and turned to him, handing him a glass of dreamwine at the same time, "There you go, a glass of dreamwine. You must know that I can't be here forever, and here it is tiring. We see all, hear all, so we would receive all the joy of all the creatures, but bear the pain of all the mortal beings. It is worse than you could ever imagine, but it is important for an overseer to ensure everything is working properly in the realm and it is time for a successor."

Mirdaff nodded. He did not fully understand all Mizervon said, but he decided he would not bother Mizervon anymore. They drank the dreamwine in silence, and Mirdaff let the sweet scent of the wine run through his mouth. Dreamwine was very rare and Mirdaff decided to treasure every moment the wine was in his mouth.

"Can you show me where Kilfer is?" Mirdaff spoke after a long time, suddenly remembering his friend.

"Oh, oh yeah sure," Mizervon was still halfway through a sip of dreamwine, "You must be quite worried for him, aren't you?"

He uttered something, then a blue screen appeared in front of them, forming the image of Kilfer...

***

Kilfer flew higher into the sky.

Flying had never been easier, and he was able to relax during his flight, and with his newly acquired magic he seemed unstoppable, and can see and hear everything a million miles from where he was. Yet, he felt it the moment he tried to feel for the presence of magic, the darkness corrupting his thoughts and blurring his vision, the abominable force that made him shudder.

The landscape changed fast beneath him, and he was soon accustomed to the roaring of the wind and frost-biting temperatures, probably because he had his magic to shield him from the environment he was in. Kilfer could feel the presence of darkness increasing, and he was anxious. Even gaining all the powers from Mizervon, Kilfer was still new to those and did not know how to use it.

Soon, cities came into view beneath him, some glowing with magic and in other cities and villagers he could sense fear in almost every being's hearts. It was clear, that they know about the arrival of the darkness.

And they are preparing.

From the distance near the horizon, a dark mass gathered, spreading through the land like contaminated water. Every plant or animal they touched turned into darkness, like shadows with a lethal touch.

"Kilfer, we meet again. I thought I would never have to see you again!" A voice deep and hollow echoed in his mind. It was coming from the darkest reaches of the darkness, of a figure that had a million countenances, with powers surpassing a thousand wizards and the savagery to spill blood across the lands, and Kilfer remembered. It was the very soulless creature that took her sister's and the Pack's life.

It was the Ghost.

"Long time no see," Kilfer replied in his mind to the Ghost, "You have become stronger."

"So have you, I see. Adopted Mizervon's powers, have you?" The Ghost smirked, "Yet you are untrained, rash and easy to kill."

The Ghost receded from his thoughts. Kilfer glanced back to one of the cities closest to the darkness and decided he would land there.

The land grew larger as he descended, and soon he could see people leaving from the back gate of the city, while there were a few men in aquamarine robes and staffs and wands. When Kilfer was young, he knew of human wizards but never knew he could see one in person, but when he could he noticed he was a wizard himself.

As he was about to land, one of the wizards spotted him and aimed his staff and Kilfer, a ball of light appearing at the tip of his wand, ready to strike.

"What monster are you?" He bellowed as Kilfer landed finally onto the ground, "Show yourself!"

"I am not a monster," Kilfer spoke, slowly revealing the seal of the Pack on his hand, "I am the human leader of the Pack, the descendant of Mizervon the great wizard who succeeded in defeating the dark forces a millennium ago."

"You're... our savior?" The wizard spoke in disbelief, slowly putting his wand down.

"Not quite a savior, but I am here to assist you against the darkness, Kilfer is my name," Kilfer spoke, eyeing the oncoming darkness, "We have no time to waste, the darkness is arriving."

"Marr, the Elder Wizard of Eltbourgh, the city of glass walls at your command," A relieved smile spread over his face, but

Kilfer himself might not be as relieved for he was not as strong as the wizards imagined him to be. Everywhere, wizards and soldiers were rushing forward to the city walls with staffs, cannons and magical arrows with them. Yet, Kilfer knew that to deal damage to the darkness, they needed far more weapons than that.

He glanced behind him, where all the buildings of Eltbourgh shimmered with light from the sun, with all the glass walls and dazzling beauty. Yet he knew that soon it would be no more when the darkness arrives. Taking a deep breath, he started walking towards the castle walls.

The waves of darkness rippled forward, cutting through all the green trees and forests, the mists let any living being shrivel into nothingness, stealing its lifeforce. Dead trees and branches and twigs and remnants of buildings from faraway cities that fell to the wrath of the darkness swirled in the misty darkness, toyed around by the unseen powers. The darkness was coming, closing on them every second. There were only two choices -- attack, or stay at the mercy of the darkness.

"What do we do now, Master Kilfer?" Marr spoke beside him, "All the wizards here are under your command."

Kilfer was not really accustomed to how Marr called him but decided not to ponder on it so much. He glanced around and found that none of the weapons were good for an offensive, and he decided it would be better if they tried to hold the city for as long as possible.

"Hold the castle walls. Create the strongest magic barrier possible," Kilfer made his decision.

"What?" Marr did not seem to be too relieved, "We defend... not attack?"

"Yes. We are in no shape to attack now, you will shield all of us while I try to deal some damage. It won't be easy to even defend," Kilfer said, "Oh, and also prepare a portal to evacuate just in case."

"The... preparations will be made," Marr spoke with some reluctance and left. Kilfer glanced back at the horizon where the darkness brewed. He had no choice, for the wizards already proclaimed him to lead the battle, yet they were not prepared, and they had to retreat in the end. The years of war from Mizervon was in his mind, the memories of every victory and every defeat in his mind, and he knew well they could not stand long.

The battle horns sounded, loud and long from both of Kilfer's sides. The battle was just beginning.

In front of the castle walls, magical shields were formed and Kilfer also weaved his own shields, and when the first waves of darkness hit the shields they were repelled, but dark misty faces emerged from the swelling darkness and impaled their teeth in the shields. Kilfer felt the tension tugging on his shield and weakening it, but with Mizervon's magic, he could still hold his own.

The greenish hue of the shields reached up to the skies as little impish figures surged out, like mere shadows yet their scarlet eyes told him otherwise. They held green fire, which was powerful enough to parry magic in combat, and seared their shields with the fire.

"Continue holding the shields! Do we have any offensive weapons? Like magic arrows or something?" Kilfer yelled and someone yelled back, "No, Master Kilfer! We only have shields!"

"Someone, protect me with your shields, I'll need to attack somehow!" Kilfer yelled, and three wizards weaved their shields in front of him. Gathering a wave of his newly acquired magic, Kilfet hurled it down from the clouds and a massive green lightning struck the dark waves, causing them to recoil and from within sharp squealing noises that hurt their ears.

The darkness receded, but as they were relieved Kilfer saw a whole new threat appearing, larger and more fearsome ap-peared -- a massive figure at least ten times the height and size of the castle walls, wielding a club the glowed an eerie crimson hue. Behind it, the dark waves did not advance, knowing his presence, but Kilfer knew somewhere within, the Ghost was there, slowly weakening them until the final, lethal blow.

The club that the figure wielded swung with a massive force, biting deep into the shields. The blow shook the shields, and Kilfer yelled to the wizards, "Keep the shields, but retreat! Get to another city that is safe through the portals!"

The wizards retreated back, and now there were only the shields to protect him, but he was sure he could destroy the hulking monster. A sword materialized in his hand and he leaped forward, out of the shields, using his magic to propel him further into the air and drew an arc through the air, slicing through the figure's chest. Dodging a quick blow from its club, the creature split into half, spewing black gore everywhere.

Kilfer landed smoothly, but he noticed the darkness advancing again and the shields dissipating fast. Green balls of fire were thrust out of the dark mist at superhuman speeds, and one caught Kilfer, hitting him hard and he would have died without his magic with him.

Kilfer felt the salty fresh blood from between his teeth, and his chest was throbbing with pain. Struggling, he drew another portal and linked to a mental connection with Marr, speaking to him.

"Where did you leave for?"

"A little more than twenty-eight miles South from here, at the city of Diamerkus. Our wizardry superweapons are all there, it will be the perfect city to prepare, " The reply came, fast and hasty.

Kilfer knew where to go to. Finally, with a burst of strength he leaped through the portal, and as the portal closed the darkness raged on, consuming all that remained.

Chapter 22

"Is there any way to communicate with Ferhia's soul?" Mirdaff asked Mizervon. They had seen all the destruction that happened in Eltbourgh, and Mirdaff hoped Kilfer was alright. Night had just set in, and Mizervon led him to their room, and they were still walking through a corridor that led from the main hall to their room.

"Only if she wants to talk," Mizervon replied, "But why did you ask?"

"I mean... she might know something, and she might have the magic to assist Kilfer."

"What? So she wields magic?" Mizervon paused in his footsteps, "Why didn't you tell me earlier?"

"She helped Kilfer before, but she could use her magic to guarantee Kilfer safety," Mirdaff said.

"You do have a point. Let's find out," Mizervon nodded, and drew a portal with his finger, "Come, this leads to where Ferhia is lying now."

They passed through it to a small, dimly-lit room, and there was nothing except for Ferhia's body, cold and her skin was pale, and her soul within her mortal shell was the only thing that prevented her mortal self from decay.

"Here, sit beside me," Mizervon instructed as the wizard sat before the corpse. Mirdaff followed and Mizervon spoke chants that sounded so eerie that Mirdaff seemed to feel a tingling sensation on his spine. As the chants continued, Ferhia's body started to glow, from a dull purplish hue to a bright sapphire glow that illuminated the entire room. Mirdaff knew that Mizervon saw the change, but the chants still continued.

After a few moments, the glow transformed into something unexpected, and a figure rose out of the light, and Mizervon stopped abruptly in his chants. Then all was silent until Ferhia's ghost spoke.

"Why did you call me?"

"About Kilfer, your brother. You know that he is in peril, and his life is at stake now..." Mizervon spoke.

"You want me to try saving him? I can't, the darkness does not allow me to."

"What do you mean? You're in the Hall of the Seven Kings, you're safe. You do have magic to help him, do you?" Mirdaff piped up.

"They are still trapping me wherever I go. It's no use. But I can tell you something else that you might want to know."

"What is it?"

"You cannot tell Kilfer about it, or the Ghost will kill me but... I can tell you the only weakness of the Ghost."

***

Kilfer lay on a bed, soft bell chimes ringing. His body hurt, but it had already subsided a lot and was left with a dull throb.

His eyes opened and struggled to get up. There was no one in sight, and he was in a room that was made from wood from the ceiling to the floorboards. The door was ajar, and he walked slowly towards the door. His body felt quite cumbersome but he managed to reach the door and pushed the door lightly. It swung open and in front of him was a walkway and he found that he was in some sort of a wizardry training school.

Around him, there were people of all ages wielding staffs and wands, and when he glanced beyond the walkway he there was a huge street filled with people and shops. Night had just fallen, and Kilfer stood at the walkway, glanced down to the bustling street below.

"Master Kilfer," Someone called him from behind. He turned, and found Marr standing behind him, "We are at Diamerkus now, you were lying on a street unconscious when I found you, you should have some more rest. We are now at the Wizardry Institution of Diamerkus, the Elder Wizards here are already informed of our presence, so we are safe here."

"My injuries are not a problem, I can heal myself. But about the darkness... how much time do we have left to prepare?"

"The surrounding cities have strong magic wielders, and they will buy us some time. The darkness would reach here by tomorrow noon, maybe tomorrow evening if we're lucky. But we are prepared, magic arrows, lots of green fire, shields and lava cannons, with a superweapon that can control lightning from the heavens, all that you can name! We will be fine, just take a stroll through the city and familiarize yourself with this new environment, the civilians will be evacuated by dawn."

Kilfer nodded and Marr left, leaving him alone at the walkway. He decided to take a quick stroll in the streets below and sauntered to the stairs at the end of the walkway.

Kilfer strolled on aimlessly, his body did not hurt at all now, but every footstep seemed so heavy. Everything seemed usual now, but by dawn all the people he saw here would most likely have evacuated, leaving simply an empty ghost of a city for them to defend.

The presence of light magic was strong in this city, and Kilfer felt it. He felt safety and comfort among all those people, and it washed all the fear and insecurity away from him.

"Selling swords! High-quality swords!" A bellow drew him away from his thoughts. Swords were always his favourite weapon, and the huge crowd drew him closer. He had created swords when he was with the Pack before, and he loved handling with short swords, but the Alpha always wanted his swords unsheathed so he had no choice and it could not be used to hunt.

Kilfer jostled his way to the front of the crowd and their swords of different sizes were placed on a red cloth on the floor, and he immediately had his eyes on a short sword with a green gem on its hilt. The blade glowed a yellow hue, and Kilfer sensed that it was different from the other swords -- it encapsulated magic.

"Sir," Kilfer walked up to the man running the stall, and jabbed at the sword, "This short sword... how much does it cost?"

"Three thousand gold coins," He replied, eyeing him warily.

"I don't have coins... but I have something you might consider to trade for," Kilfer searched his tunic pocket, and took out a piece of ice. It was the never-melting ice, and he got it from his travel to Mizervon, and he never thought that he could use it.

"The never-melting ice -- or what you call it," Kilfer held it in front of the man, "It's rare enough you could take a thousand men to exchange for it. Trade this ice for your sword. Deal?"

"Deal," Came the immediate reply.

***

"His eyes. The only mortal part is its eyes. But it is incredibly hard -- almost impossible to reach it for he never shows his face. You can never see his face, and if you could his eyes will glare at you to make even the strongest of ordinary wizards melt before even striking a blow on his eyes," Ferhia's ghost said, "And I also have another secret, and you should be informed about it."

"We're listening," Mizervon spoke.

"Tomorrow, the dark forces will clash with Kilfer's wizards. And the Ghost is using me as a bait, and he will use my ghost to fight Kilfer. I can't stop it, for I am simply a doll in the Ghost's hands."

Ferhia's image disappeared before them, and Mizervon stood, looking less than relieved, "Kilfer's life is in his own hands, but I have to help him in some way or another. He is in no shape to face the Ghost on his own, for the Ghost is far more powerful than he had ever been before."

***

It was morning. The dawn had just broken, and there was an annoying silence; he could not even hear the sound of a bird tweet or the whistle of the wind.

Kilfer's sword was beside him as he strolled the empty streets of Diamerkus. The light snow added on to the serenity, but he knew soon after there would be no peace, only war, in the city.

The night before he had gone to bed early, and he dreamt of the Pack, the Alpha, its white fur and aquamarine eyes that gave him a sense of security.

"Master Kilfer," A voice interrupted his thoughts and he turned to see Marr and another wizened old man approximately the same age as Marr himself.

"We've been searching for you when we saw you were not at your room. We need to discuss a few things for the battle.

This is Eglish, the Elder Wizard of Diamerkus," Marr spoke, introducing the other wizard.

"So what do you ask of me?" Mirdaff spoke as they sauntered through the snow-filled streets.

"We need someone with magic strong enough to power the superweapon. It will be positioned at the Wizardry Institution of Diamerkus, you'll spot it at your first glance, it's huge. But you won't be able to fight the darkness face to face," Eglish spoke, turning to Kilfer in spite, "We, of course, can handle the battle ourselves."

Kilfer did not reply. He thought about it carefully. He had the choice, and he could object, for all the wizards would perish. The darkness is worse and stronger than any wizard can take on. He could summon spirits, and use it against the darkness. The spirits of the Pack were in his hands, he could summon them to fight the darkness anytime and using the spirits were important to be able to do considerable damage to the darkness, and he decided he would tell the truth an object.

Kilfer paused in his tracks, and spoke, gazing right at Eglish, "I'm sorry. The darkness is far worse than you could ever imagine in your wildest dreams. Leaving the darkness to fight you will mean death for all of us. I must stay on the front line."

"How dare you disobey me! I am the Elder Wizard here, you should be listening to my orders," Eglish spoke coldly.

"A mere wizard you are. I am the descendant of Mizervon and human leader of the Pack. I hope you will obey, this is for your own good," Kilfer spoke in vengeance. He did not know why these words leaped out of his mouth but decided this is simply his pure agitation.

"You..." Anger burnt in Eglish's eyes, but Kilfer remained calm, and finally, Marr interrupted them, clearly noticing the anger between them, "Okay, calm down, it's not much to squabble about, we still have an entire war to fight! Master Kilfer, I respect your decision, you can stay on the front lines, but you still have to obey the Master Eglish's commands during the battle."

Kilfer did not want to say anymore. The wizards don't know anything. They think they are skilled, but they do not know the wrath of the darkness. He reached out and felt the darkness, barely a few miles away, and noticed a smaller but powerful force of light magic fighting against the darkness, and it was clear that it is a neighboring city. They could buy time, but Kilfer had to do his own preparations. Ignoring Eglish and waving goodbye to Marr, Kilfer strode on to a spot he saw yesterday while strolling across the street, a small piece of grassland covered on all four corners with tall bushes.

The perfect discreet place that no one would know of his presence there. Kilfer reached deep into his magic and found the magic to summon the Alpha's ghost. He tugged on the magic and in front of him the Alpha appeared, its snowy white fur was still as graceful and noble as ever, its deep azure eyes staring deep into him, and the moment their gazes met, a lot of feelings poured out of him, and he could feel the same in the Alpha. He felt guilty, to have the Alpha die and he could not do anything about it, the grief and the sadness in him, the Alpha and both of them intertwined.

"I'm sorry," Kilfer spoke, and found himself choked with sorrow and his cheeks were wet with tears, "Please don't blame Ferhia. But forgive me. I failed you. I failed the Pack. I'm sorry."

The Alpha nodded with understanding, speaking in his mind, "I will never blame you, Kilfer. I know that you love Ferhia as a sister, and I will always be assisting you. Whenever you need me."

"Really?" Kilfer smiled, "I have a request... it will be hard but you will not regret it. It will be for the honor of the Pack and revenge for the Pack... and a few others..."

"You can call on me anytime, just summon me and the Pack will help you to the best of our ability," The Alpha spoke in his mind, and Kilfer released his grasp on the Alpha's ghost and the Alpha faded into nothingness.

Kilfer came out of the hiding spot and pretended nothing happened, but he felt that the darkness was much closer now, its presence overshadowing the city. Time was limited for them, and he knew he had to get to the city walls before darkness' arrival.

Kilfer hastened his steps as he continued through the empty streets of the city and finally reached the castle walls. Most of the ballista was already positioned on the walls, and Kilfer tightened his grip on his sword. This was his first battle, but also the most important battle that might change the course of the entire realm.

He scaled the stairs that led up to the top of the walls and saw the pots of steaming green fire and magic arrows that sizzled with energy, and beyond the walls were huge mountains that reached up to the clouds.

"Master Kilfer," A young wizard strode up to him, "Nice to meet you, Milrend is my name, and I am sent by Marr to assist you."

"Oh, nice to meet you too," Kilfer smiled back, "By the way, who is in charge of the preparations here?"

"Master Eglish, if you wanted to know," Milrend replied.

"Oh, him," Kilfer's face fell at his name. He had never liked him from the start and decided Eglish would give him trouble even during the war.

"Just bear with Master Eglish," Milrend spoke, smiling forcefully and seemed to know what Kilfer was thinking about, "He might be really annoying sometimes, but he is quite caring to all of us, it's just that he does not show it."

Kilfer rose an eyebrow in scorn but did not say anything more. He wanted to focus on the battle and he needed to win this war, but this victory meant more to him than anyone in the realm for reasons he kept to himself, and he could take his own life if it was needed to win the war.

"Master Kilfer," Milrend said again, "I have some instructions from Master Marr for you to activate the crystal needed to activate the wizardry superweapon, for you are the only one who can gather nature's spirit into the crystal."

"And where is it?"

"Here, follow me," Milrend brought him down the castle wall to a few wizards who were waiting with a box.

"Here, it's inside the box," Milrend gestured for Kilfer to open the box and he lifted the lid. Inside, the crystal glowed a dull yellowish hue. Kilfer reached out and placed his hand on the stone, grasping the Nature's spirit from the deepest within his magic and sent it out, from deep within him to the tip of his fingers and into the crystal.

The crystal shone immediately, its dazzling golden hue seemed like the bright light from dawn, and Kilfer released his touch on the crystal.

"There," Kilfer spoke, noticing how dry his mouth suddenly became. That very instant where he dived deep to pull out Nature's spirit exhausted him from head to toe, "Bring it back, the crystal is ready."

***

Mizervon the Ancient sighed. Normally dreamwine would have cured all the worries he had, but this time his heart was still burdened with guilt and fear. If he had trained Kilfer a little more, his experience and skills might save him from certain death. But now he was untrained and young, and he was rash, and that was his nature. With a bait like using Ferhia's ghost against Kilfer, it could easily take his life.

The hall was silent as always, and Mirdaff was still asleep in his room. He stood from the chair at the side of the hall and struggled towards the center of the hall, and knelt before the statue of the Wolf God.

"Please, your holiness, forgive me. This decision I will make, for the good of the realm," Mizervon spoke within his heart.

Taking a deep breath, he stood. His final decision had been made, and it will come with a price but his sacrifice will be worth everything.

"Master Mizervon?" Mirdaff spoke behind him.

"Oh, oh you are awake?" Mizervon turned and beckoned to him to the altar. Mirdaff walked towards Mizervon as the wizard took out three capsules from behind the altar.

"Here, Mirdaff. After sunset, eat one of this, and go to where Ferhia's body lay and place the second capsule into her mouth. For the third one, give it to Kilfer when he returns. After sunset, after you have done all of these, do not go out of your room. Not until the next sunrise," Mizervon placed the capsules on Mirdaff's hands, "These are the last immortality pills, and when -- or if -- Ferhia's curse is broken she can then be immortal. Take it and don't lose it, for it is worth more than a thousand jewels. Trust me, you will all be safe."

Mizervon ushered a surprised Mirdaff back to his room. He had to be fast, for sunset will be when he shall prepare the sacrifice...

***

Kilfer felt that the darkness was very near.

The mountains were still, and there was no sign of movement, yet it was tense on the city walls. Kilfer stood in the middle, watching the mountains beyond for any sign of movement.

"I don't think that the darkness would be arriving so early, we don't have to prepare --" Milrend raised an eyebrow, but paused as Kilfer silenced him.

"They may come anytime. I can sense it --" Kilfer spoke right before a horn sounded in the distance and an entire piece of land on a mountain caved in, and revealed a huge gaping hole and thousands of soldiers whose skin was shadowy-black and seemed only like shadows on the ground but every living being that touched it -- including the smallest ants and grass and flowers and bees -- shrivelled up into lifeless beings, and every kill nourished their power, making them larger, more powerful than ever. From behind the mountains, dark mists flowed like water, covering the mountains in shadowy darkness.

Yet what Kilfer feared most was the lone figure that led the army of shadows, even though she was cloaked in darkness, Kilfer would never have mistaken her.

Ferhia.

Kilfer immediately realized what was happening and stood there in shock. He never expected the darkness to turn Ferhia against him, and glanced at Eglish. His eyes stared motionlessly at the oncoming darkness, and all the archers ready. The darkness was getting closer, nearly within firing range of the arrows, but if those arrows with green fire were to hit Ferhia, she would die immediately.

Eglish signaled for the archers to get ready, and hundreds of them lining the castle walls pulled on the bowstring.

"Wait!" Kilfer yelled, and although he was not that loud Eglish was merely a few feet beside him and he turned, and his gaze met Kilfer's, "Don't shoot yet. There are some... personal issues I have to deal with."

"You deal with what you want to do, but if you die my archers are going to fire," Master Eglish said, eyeing Kilfer suspiciously. Kilfer knew that Master Eglish did not trust him, but said no more.

The shadowy troops stopped behind Ferhia when they saw Kilfer come down from the city walls. Everyone was not moving at all, their eyes fixated on both Ferhia and Kilfer.

"You still have a chance of control on yourself. Please wake up, Ferhia. Don't let them control you..." Kilfer spoke but paused when Ferhia drew a sword that emanated a sharp black glow around it.

Kilfer sighed and shook his head. He drew his blade, and the yellowish glow of the blade enveloped him.

"You leave me with no choice, my sister. Forgive me," Kilfer spoke, but he knew that he could not kill his sister. But he will find a way around it.

Then Ferhia attacked. Their blades hit each other, and it was then Kilfer realized how powerful the darkness had made Ferhia become. Their blades, dark and light, danced through the air in a flurry of motion, and Kilfer finally had a plan. The only way is for Kilfer to grab her hand and from there, enter her inner self and turn her soul to his side. But given Ferhia's dart-like accuracy and speed, he could not reach her hand, and the only thing he could possibly do -- was to lose.

Kilfer swung his blade lightly and Ferhia blocked it with her sword using so much strength Kilfer's sword skidded out of his hands -- just as he wanted. There was a risk, but that was the only thing he could do.

Kilfer could see Ferhia smirk, and she let down her guard and dropped her sword on the ground in contempt. From the tip of her finger, Ferhia ignited a ball of yellow energy and directed it at Kilfer.

"Fear the darkness," A raspy voice that was not hers growled from inside, and she was about to make the lethal blow when Kilfer leaped up and held tight onto Kilfer's hands, forcing his lifeforce into her inner self. Then time stopped on the battlefield, but amidst all the sudden calm Kilfer needed to fight a battle of her own...

***

The dark tendrils in Ferhia's inner self were growing longer, thicker every second, coiling around Ferhia's inner self, locking her within folds of darkness. Her eyes were closed, and she was still and unmoving. Kilfer dropped his sword, but now he recalled his sword the very last moment before he entered her inner self and it was now in his hands.

Lifting his sword, Kilfer leaped up and stabbed a tendril and it sizzled into nothingness. The rest of the tendrils, sensing that there was an intruder, attacked, extending towards him at an amazing speed. The tendrils sizzled in the air, sparks, and heat frying the air around them.

Kilfer parried every attack, slicing through the shadowy darkness. The sword seemed weightless as his magic took over, slashing at any that dared come near, but he knew that his time was limited. The tendrils were extending at such a fast rate that he would soon be encircled, and all he had to do is to wake Ferhia out of the trance she was helplessly falling into, and she was barely a dozen feet away from him. He had to reach Ferhia and wake her before he faced the same fate as her, like how she saved him from his dream at the Lair of the Ghost.

He yelled a battle cry and lumbered forward, and swung his sword in all directions, and all around him sparks flew as the blade scraped the tendrils, and he fended off all but one, which attacked him from behind, coiling around both of his wrists. The pain seared him from his skin, biting into his flesh and bones. Kilfer winced and felt the strength within him ebbing every second the dark tendrils clung onto him. With a last, violent movement, Kilfer sent a wave of light from within his body and felt the darkness melting around him, but he could not sustain the magic long enough and Ferhia was barely three steps away from him, and he leaped forward, grabbing Ferhia's shoulder and yelled, "Ferhia, wake up!"

The wave of light magic from Kilfer had already dispersed, and the darkness was closing on him. Ferhia had no response, but Kilfer knew that if he yielded and let the darkness encapsulate him, it would be death, and they would have no hope.

"Ferhia, please! Wake up!" Kilfer yelled with only that small amount of hope that Ferhia would wake up from the trance, but the hope was dissipating. The dark tendrils were already around him, getting closer every second, ready to send a lethal strike around him. Kilfer shut his eyes tight, praying all the verses to the Wolf God that he could, and focusing on Ferhia, hoping that she would escape from the iron fist of the darkness...

Then the entire inner self of Ferhia shook. It was merely a tiny shudder, but both Kilfer and the darkness felt it, and the dark tendrils stiffened warily. Kilfer opened his eyes slowly and looked at Ferhia. From that mere tremor, Kilfer felt that Ferhia was trying to escape, and he used his own magic to aid her, passing all the magic that his strength could manage into her inner self, and another tremor rocked her inner self, and soon the tremors in the ground turned into violent shaking, with the darkness trying to control Ferhia and Ferhia trying to break the curse the darkness had over her.

"Please, Ferhia," Kilfer spoke, slowly and cautiously, and he knew somewhere within her there was a free part of her body who was listening, "You are stronger than anyone can ever imagine, this is your inner self, and no power can stop you in here. Wake up."

Then, Ferhia's coal black eyes flung open, and it released a force so strong that it flung Kilfer far out into the air until he was soaring up, and from above he could see the dark tendrils evaporating, then a ray of light took over. Kilfer squinted and could not see anything, then the next moment he was sprawled on the ground, back on the battlefield. More than a million eyes were staring at him, and Ferhia was nowhere to be seen.

Kilfer stood, and faced the army of darkness, and he felt uncertainty within the masses of shadows. They were afraid, he realized. The heartless, merciless beings who lived off blood were fearful.

Then, Kilfer turned back to face his own kind, the archers, wizards and all that guarded the city, "We have won our first battle against the darkness. They are not invincible, and we will drive the darkness away! Hiding behind the walls is of no use, come out and fight, and we will prevail!"

As he spoke, he noticed that behind him, the masses of warriors were swarming towards him, and they had limited time before the darkness was to consume them. There were only two choices -- to fight or to die.

Then, Master Eglish rose into the air, and yelled the command Kilfer would never forget, "Follow Kilfer! Fight to the end!"

From the castle walls, hundreds of wizards and warriors leaped down, wielding the spears and swords and hammers glowing full of magic. Kilfer smiled and summoned the entire Pack, and the souls of wolves drifted up from beneath the ground and joined the wizards, the Alpha standing beside him.

In a single fluid motion, Kilfer leaped upon the Alpha's back and held his sword high into the air, "Attack!"

The Alpha and Kilfer charged into the sea of darkness and slashed on all the dark soldiers, and from their sides the rest of the Pack attacked, then the wizards, who flung blasts of magic at the darkness.

Swords, staffs and battle axes clashed, and alongside him, he saw wizards killed by the darkness, heads rolling and blood spilling everywhere. A sword scraped his shin, drawing blood and Kilfer winced, slashing the soldier with all his might, multiple times until the soldier collapsed into the shadows. A volley of arrows shot from the city walls; raining on the darkness and green fire erupted, consuming all the darkness that stood in its path.

Seeing yet another wizard fall to the swords wielded by the darkness, Kilfer knew that sacrifices had to be made. There was hope -- but the war was far from over.

Then, from the dark mists behind the battlefield a wave of darkness rippled out, the purest -- but deadliest -- dark magic that existed, and he could feel its menace as it arrived, and he knew they would all be wiped out if the dark wave hit them.

"Hey," Kilfer whispered in Wolf tongue into the Alpha's ears, "Continue fighting, I need to deal with something important."

The Alpha nodded quickly, and Kilfer soared above the battlefield. Kilfer reached deep into his magic, deeper than ever before until he found something beyond, that all magic seemed to be connected to it. It was white, pure and gave off a radiance that he had never felt or seen before. Closing his eyes, he reached out to the magic and felt the strength surge into him, from his arms to the tip of his finger, until the magic burst out of his fingertips with such strength he was nearly thrown off balance, and he squinted his eyes as he watched the blinding light surge towards the darkness and a moment later they collided with such force the mountains, the waters, and even the air shook, and after it all there was silence.

The entire battlefield was silent, the Pack, wizards and dark forces staring at what was left from the blast -- a huge grey blob of magic hovering in the air, showering sparks occasionally in all directions. At his first glance, Kilfer could tell that the magic was unstable, and could explode at any moment if triggered by anything, possibly even by the smallest flutter of a wing.

The entire battlefield was silent, and no one moved an inch, and all -- whether the dark or the light -- feared for their lives. However, all forgot one thing that Kilfer suddenly remembered when a huge blast shook the ground from behind the castle walls, and blasts of lightning shot out from the Crystal, the wizardry superweapon that they owned, and one shot right at the glowing grey ball of energy! Certainly, those that controlled the superweapon from within the city did not know about all that was happening on the battlefield, and would not know that the action of firing the Crystal could take their lives.

"Run!" Kilfer yelled and the wizards took to their heels, and all of a sudden all the wizards and the Pack were retreating back to the castle walls, with Kilfer riding the wind back to the city walls. However, the dark troops were stranded, unable to return back within the dark mists and Kilfer did not know what would become of them, but the next moment he glanced back after reaching the safety of the city the troops were decimated by the blast, and wizards that were not fast enough were also killed, their steaming bodies left on the ground.

"Master Kilfer, thank you," Milrend spoke beside him, watching the catastrophe while the rest of the wizards leaped up the castle walls to safety, "We won all because of you -- and the Pack."

"But we're far from a full victory, the darkness still prevails," Kilfer smiled and said, but he knew the decisive victory came at a price. There were not more than a hundred wizards left on the city walls, and more than half of the wizards perished in simply a single battle. He also wondered if he should leave the dark troops to die. They simply wished for freedom from behind the veil and were simply puppets of the Ghost. Maybe if he saved them their loyalty would change, and they would turn to the good. They felt fear, and they had feelings, and he questioned himself if the darkness was actually evil and if the light was actually good. Maybe, one day the light and the dark could live harmoniously. Maybe...

Watching the dark mists retreat back to behind the mountains, Kilfer felt uncertain about the battle, and what would become of it...

***

Mizervon prepared the ritual.

It was nearly midnight, and he knelt before the statue of the Wolf God. Mirdaff was in his room, and he was relieved that it would all finally end. The cold bluish glow of the moonlight showered into the hall as Mizervon raised the ritual dagger. In the ancient, most sacred language of the Wolf Tongue, he spoke:

O mighty god of a million wolves:

This sacrifice I shall make, My lifeforce to nourish my young successor,

For yet another victory against the heartless darkness.

This sacrifice I shall make,

For the lives of billions and yet more to come,

And for the ever-lasting, almighty good,

I shall take my life for Kilfer,

One worthy of my place.

Then, with a fluid motion, he swung the dagger onto his chest, and after that, a mere silence took over...

Chapter 23

The night that came after the battle was a sleepless night. Only at dawn did Kilfer manage to sleep for barely an hour before he was rudely interrupted by a rushed, loud series of knocks on his door. Kilfer groggily stood, and muttered barely loud enough for the person outside to hear him, "Come in."

The door barged open and there Marr stood, his face pale with fear, "Master Kilfer! We need your help, there is another attack now, the remaining dark soldiers and other demons are destroying our city walls and killing our wizards, we can't hold them for long!"

Kilfer's eyes widened, grabbed his sword lying at the corner of his room and strode outside, "Come, let's go."

Both wizards flew towards the wall, and Kilfer immediately realized that the forces were more and much deadlier than the previous attack. Besides the mere troops which could be easily destroyed with usual wizardry weapons, the demons that usually hid behind the mists of darkness were out huge dark giants who were demolishing the wall and heads that hovered within the air and delivered blasts of purple magic to destroy the archers on the wall. Behind everything, Kilfer saw the true nightmare, the nightmare that was real, and right in front of them.

However, the looming figure had only its massive hands extending out of the dark mists, and with every movement of his hands the demons attacked, and Kilfer quickly realise that the Ghost was controlling them, and by destroying the Ghost would allow the demons to be unorganized and would lead them to victory, although that was nearly impossible.

Kilfer and Marr landed on the wall as the first troops reached the top of the wall. Kilfer drew his sword and the dance of blades began. With his magic, Kilfer handled his sword with such fluidity that the sword seemed to become part of him, and he cut and killed many. A sword cut him on the thigh deep enough for blood to stain his tunic red, but he continued. He suddenly felt that he could not feel pain, and only an immortal being could do so, and when Kilfer glanced down the wound was healed. Kilfer felt the difference, he was suddenly far stronger than he was the night before, and even if he trained the entire night he could not become an immortal or anything near it. Unless...

A wave of magic came directly at him and hit him, and he was caught off-guard and sent him falling onto the floor, his sword skidding out of his reach. When he tried to stand up, two dark soldiers were already on him, lifting their swords, one preparing to cut his neck and the other to embed its sword into his heart, and both had the nightmarish red eyes and lunatic grin, and he knew no one -- not even an immortal could survive a stab to the neck or heart. Kilfer swiftly landed a kick on one of the soldiers and sent a blast of magic onto the face of another. The magic hit him in the face and it burned, and the last Kilfer heard was the soldier's cries of pain until it died into a pile of black, smoking goo. The other soldier tried to attack him but he dodged just as the soldier planted his sword down and reached for his sword, and used magic to pull it to his grasp and parried the other hit, and they fought on the edge of the wall. Kilfer tried using his magic but the dark soldier dodged every hit and he noticed that he was a much harder opponent than the rest. Yet, he was no match for Kilfer. Kilfer sidestepped an attack, and pushed him off the wall. The last thing he heard from the soldier was the echoes of the his scream as he plummeted down the wall.

Another tried to stab him from behind, but Kilfer shot a blast of magic that seared its face and with a swift stroke he landed a lethal cut to the throat, and blood spurted on his face.

He glanced around. They were already heavily outnumbered, and with the many demons destroying the wall it would be soon before they perished.

"Wizards! Gather back, we're retreating!" Kilfer yelled and the surviving wizards glided into the air, and he could see that there were a mere twenty of the wizards left, and a few archers who the wizards helped lift into the air, and all were hurt, their shins, arms and faces filled with cuts, bruises and their tunic stained with blood.

"Back to the Wizardry Institution!" Kilfer glided into the air and dived down towards the Wizardry Institution, the huge building was the only building to serve as a wall against the demons. Kilfer spoke to Master Eglish, "Protect the super-weapon, and use it against the demons. You have to trust me here, I need to fight someone else."

Eglish took a deep breath and nodded, "I trust you, go to what you need to fight, we will try to stay alive."

***

Kilfer rode the winds back to the remains of the city walls. The demons had already broken in, and he tried to evade from their view by hiding behind a building. After they left, he glided down to the remains of the castle wall and stood, facing the Ghost.

"Well, well, well," The Ghost came out of the dark mist, sitting atop an obsidian throne, "You have gotten stronger, I see. But a rash young soul is what Mizervon sent to fight me after these years?"

"Face me! Do not even underestimate me, not today," Kilfer spoke. He found that he could not bring himself to face his eyes yet again, however, he was prepared. He would not lose to the Ghost another time. Not today. He raised his sword slowly and gathered magic into his sword.

"Then let's see what can you do," The Ghost spoke with spite. Kilfer attacked, slashing his sword through the air and the magic within his sword was unleashed, sending a wave of magic slicing through the air towards the Ghost. The Ghost simply chortled and flicked the magic away, but Kilfer was already prepared. He dropped his sword and focused deep into his magic, and raised his arms wide. All around him, spirits of all sorts and all magic from the skies and the land reached out to his aid and the sky flashed with lightning while the ground blazed with flames. Spirits of deer, lions, bears, and even the trees with their root reaching out from beneath the ground and birds who glided up from beneath the ground. The spirits were all who fell because of the darkness, including the Pack who stood beside him. Bronswig rode on one of the wolves and grinned broadly when their gaze met. Finally, a spirit that had a glow brighter than most came up from the ground beside him, and when he turned he saw that someone had returned. She was the one that he loved the most, and she was his sister.

Ferhia.

They gazed at each other and Kilfer smiled first, speaking so silently that only both of them could hear, "Thank you for coming back, my sister."

Kilfer turned back to the Ghost, and the strength of all the spirits behind him gave him strength, "You are fed by grief, you survive on the manipulation of the darkness, you are using them, and their deaths mean nothing to you. But that way, you will never succeed. All that had fallen under your feet now have unimaginable power behind me, and you shall die. You are strong, but we are many. You shall not live today."

"We'll see," The Ghost spoke and Kilfer could hear the anger behind his calm voice. He picked up his sword and heard Ferhia whisper behind him, "Look to his face and stab his eyes. It is its only weakness."

Kilfer nodded and stepped forward. The moment he reached into his magic he noticed the difference, his entire self felt different, rejuvenated and he knew that someone else was helping him, but could not remember who would have such strong magic, but he did not have more time to think about it for the Ghost attacked, shadows extending from his fingers and trying to attack Kilfer. He parried the quick attacks and extended a blast of magic. It crackled towards the Ghost, but it did not seem to harm him, simply dissolving the moment it hit the Ghost.

From behind the spirits channeled magic into Kilfer, and he could feel himself growing stronger and stronger, but with every second that went by Kilfer was more and more certain that he might not stand a chance against the Ghost.

"Just accept your fate, you are merely delaying the inevitable," The Ghost spoke in his mind, chortling. Kilfer felt the Ghost's eyes burning into him, but he could not bring himself to look at the Ghost, and with every attack, Kilfer was tiring himself out. The Ghost shot another blast of magic and it hit Kilfer square in the ribs, he knelt in pain, and the Ghost laughed in a booming voice that echoed in his consciences as waves of torment. The Ghost stood from his massive throne and turned back to his human size, and stood in front of Kilfer mockingly.

"Kilfer, listen to me," Another voice called out in his mind which he recognized as Ferhia, "You can do it. You could not look into his eyes because we know that it is impossible, but you have the magic for the physical strength to win against him. If you remember how Mizervon had once defeated the Ghost and send attack his eyes... you will succeed."

Kilfer took a deep breath and leaped up, but instead of attacking his eyes he did something no one would expect -- he leaped into the inner self of the Ghost.

It seemed as if he was entering the trap of the Ghost, but it did not matter to him. He wanted to know why the Ghost wanted death and destruction, why it, as the leader of darkness led the rest of the darkness to the path of evil. Darkness could be good too, for he felt emotions within even the darkest devils, it was merely the Ghost who taught them evil. The moment he entered the inner self of the Ghost, however, he seemed trapped within the thick mists and fog with the stench of rotting smell that gagged him. He had never been to a place that smelt that bad, and the Swamps was far better when compared to that place. The air also seemed to hurt him, drawing his lifeforce away from him, and in around him two huge pairs of green eyes circled him.

"Why did you lead yourself into the trap that you knew you couldn't fall into?" The Ghost spoke with scorn, "I could easily kill you in here... but you must have a motive by coming here. Now tell me what do you want before I kill you, maybe your death would not be so unmeaningful."

"Why did you choose this?" Kilfer spoke. The stench and pain in its inner self was so unbearable that Kilfer's mouth was heavy and dry, and he could barely speak.

"Choose what?"

"The path of evil. Why did you lead the darkness to evil, and why do you not want the darkness and light live harmoniously as one? The darkness might not exactly be evil, and the light might not exactly be good, so why did you have to lead the darkness to become evil?" Kilfer spoke, breathing heavily.

"Ha! Now you ask this question! It was because of you, all of you who claims to be the light, the good, who sent us into the prison in the Swamps. This realm was created equal, but you light wizards abused your authority and sent us to exile. We had no choice but to turn to the face of evil to regain the balance, and even more, our revenge. But now you know the truth, and you can finally die."

A figure strode out of the darkness, and Kilfer looked up and stared at the Ghost's face, and the Ghost stepped back in shock, "How could you..."

Who Kilfer saw was merely a cold face made of white marble and its eyes were white and blind. Kilfer knew it was this that blinded him -- the seek for not only justice but power over the realm.

"You thought you were powerful, but you were consumed by the greed and thirst for revenge and power. Now, I shall end you," Kilfer spoke, planting his hands on the marble eyes of the Ghost, and from its eyes, the skin cracked, and the Ghost let out a long, loud howl that shook every bone and muscle in Kilfer. Yet, he held on, and the cracks deepened and cut through the marble face.

Then, the marble split open, the bits of stone crashing down onto the floor, and what was left was an empty robe. The Ghost had been consumed by Evil itself and had no way of returning to the good.

But the Ghost was right about one thing -- the realm was created equal. Neither can the evil be defeated, nor can the light be destroyed. The war between the two sides will rage on even long the Ghost, merely a physical manifestation of evil is destroyed. Many shall perish, but the balance between the evil and the good shall continue to exist, and never to be toppled.

***

When the exited from the Ghost's inner self, it was silent. The spirits had left, and only Ferhia remained. Beneath his feet, small chunks of marble remained and he picked the largest piece up, and there two lifeless marble eyes stared up at him. Near him, the robe of the Ghost was on the ground, tattered and torn. Behind him, the dark mists were still swirling, but without the Ghost it could be easily driven back, behind the veil.

He dropped the piece of marble and turned to face Ferhia.

"We won," Kilfer spoke, his voice shuddering, "We won."

"Not exactly," Ferhia replied, "We did not win, there were many deaths. All the spirits you summoned that aided you in defeating the Ghost, Bronswig, and all the wizards that fell. They sacrificed themselves to help you, and do you think we should call this a victory. I learned a lot when I was trapped with the darkness, they were not pure evil. Evil cannot be destroyed, but it manifests itself in all places where good exists. It is beyond comprehension, Kilfer. We are not victorious. We merely sacrificed many to fight the fears in our hearts."

Kilfet was speechless. He studied Ferhia slowly and noticed that she had changed considerably. Her hair had turned white, and her eyes seemed older than she was, and they were a knowing pair of eyes that understood him, and he chose not to speak.

"Mizervon died, too," Ferhia spoke, seeing that Kilfer was still silent, "Without you having his lifeforce we would not have survived."

"What? Mizervon..."

"He sacrificed himself to save everyone, including you, Kilfer. I know that you are heartbroken but you will receive the news sooner or later. Now go back to have some rest, and Mirdaff and I will be at the Hall of the Seven Kings expecting you," Ferhia spoke, and her spirit disappeared. Kilfer knelt, and he was heartbroken. Around him, thousands of bodies lay, and parts of the ground were burning with green fire.

Slowly, he gathered himself up and stood, every step heavier than the other. When he finally reached the Wizardry Institution, the building was ruined, and although the devils were all killed there were barely a dozen alive among all the destruction, all of them gravely wounded.

Marr took many cuts to his limbs and blood smeared his face, while Master Eglish and a couple others lay on the ground, eyes closed and lifeless. Marr smiled forcefully when he saw Kilfer, and Kilfer spoke, "Fear not, the darkness is gone. This war was never worth the casualties, but at least we annihilated the evil."

For a moment, they paused and surveyed the destruction. The city had been reduced to a desolate wasteland with crumbling buildings and the bodies of wizards and devils were strewn all over the ground. Hawks and falcons were swooping over the mess, and many started descending to eat the corpses.

"More wizards and soldiers from the rest of the realm are arriving to help in restoring this city and those beyond. It might take a couple years but it will be back to normal soon, and a proper burial will be carried for all who died in this battle," Marr said, "Stories of the Pack will definitely be told across generations, and you will be honored like Mizervon was."

Kilfer merely nodded but he was still not relieved yet. One day, the evil might once again resurface and wreak havoc across the realm. There will always be sacrifices, but the war would rage on.

***

Kilfer took off from Diamerkus, back to the Hall of the Seven Kings, and left the wizards to repair the lands. The realm would never be the same, and by taking a last glance back at the dark mists it seemed to be dissipating, and beyond Diamerkus was still a land of mesmerizing beauty of forests and lands and seas and cities where life still flourished -- at least, for now.

Kilfer never told the surviving wizards about the death of Mizervon, and he knew that his stories would be told for generations and generations to come, and he knew that when Evil manifests itself on another being again, there would be one soul like Kilfer to fight the darkness, for the balance would never be destroyed.

EPILOGUE

K ilfer landed at the Hall of the Seven Kings. Inside, everything was the same, the marble floor, the statues of the Seven Kings and the altar of the Wolf God was the same, but it bore a totally new meaning to him, one of responsibility, for he knew that he was the next human leader of the Pack to guard the Hall of the Seven Kings and become the Wolf God.

Taking a deep breath, he opened the doors and Ferhia and Mirdaff were there, and Mirdaff was the first to speak, "Kilfer, you're back!"

"Where is Master Mizervon?" Kilfer mumbled. He was far from joyful, but he must find where Mizervon's body was.

"His body is in the chamber down the hallway, but he wanted you to take this," Mirdaff took a pill out of his tunic pocket and grabbed a glass of water from the table near them and handed them to Kilfer, "The last immortality pill."

Kilfer took the pills and gulped it down his throat, and turned back to Mirdaff and Ferhia, "Come now, show me where Mizervon is."

Mirdaff led them down the hallway until they stopped at the end, and he pushed the door open. There, on a red mat Mizervon lay silent. After a thousand years, Mizervon had finally ended his suffering, his tiring contributions to fight against evil, and his usual wizened, tired eyes was replaced with calm.

Kilfer knelt beside Mizervon, and prayed to the Wolf God. Mizervon had left him forever, and he was on his own now. Although he was entirely uncertain if what would happen in the future, he knew that the blood of wolves ran in him, and the spirits of the Pack would aid him forever.

He is the Wolf Child.